James Morrison

Treehouse

The Dial Press
New York
1972

HOUSTON PUBLIC LIBRARY

Library of Congress Cataloging in Publication Data

Morrison, James, 1923–
   Treehouse.

   I.   Title.
PZ4.M88174Tr   [PS3563.O87434]   Q813'.5'4   75–37449

Printed in the United States of America

Second Printing 1972

Book design by Margaret McCutcheon

for Anne

Thus I draw from the absurd three consequences, which are my revolt, my freedom, and my passion. By the mere activity of consciousness I transform into a rule of life what was an invitation to death—

—Albert Camus
from "The Myth of Sisyphus"

Treehouse

Chapter

One

The Peace Corps has shrinks that give you a pretty thorough going over before they spend a lot of money shipping you off to the boonies. Thorough. That's a laugh. This shrink asked me if I had nightmares, and did I wet the bed, and did I like girls, and did I suck door-knobs. And then suddenly, from way out in left field, he asked me did I think much about who my real parents had been. So from short right field I gave him a quick "Nah." The interview took place late on a Friday after-noon, while the shrink was splitting his bureaucratic at-tention between me and a government-operated clock, and this last question fell when the little hand was on four and the big hand was on six. So the chitchat came to an abrupt end; the shrink went fishing, and I went to

Kumi in Uganda. That was two years ago. Now I'm back from Kumi in Uganda, and I'm riding on a bus heading for Burlington, Vermont, in the United States of America, and again I'm saying to myself that I don't think much about the fact of my adoption. And, of course, this is and was absolutely true. It's something you don't *think* about. At times you feel about it. You're aware of it. Sort of like a mole on your cheek. But you don't think about it. At least after you begin to accept what it means, you don't think about it. It's just a feeling that comes and goes, and sometimes you feel the feeling stronger than at other times. Sometimes it's like a mole on your cheek and other times it's like a boil on your butt. Nellie knows what I mean.

I'm not riding this bus because I'm impoverished. I could have taken a plane for this leg of the trip, and now that the fatigue of four days of travel has seeped into me I think perhaps I should have done so. But I wanted to see the land and what has happened to it since I've been away, and the bus seemed the most appropriate way to accomplish this. I wonder what has changed most in the two intervening years. My country or me. I'd call it a draw.

Albany is behind us now and we are getting into country that hasn't been cooked by the pressure of progress. It's shabby, yes, but not ugly. Not scarred by auto graveyards and subdivisions and all the other marvels of technology. Large farms and tiny backwater towns. Swamps and plowed fields. And it looks good and makes me feel good, and I think of the story I read somewhere that when Roosevelt was President he would draw his family together on New Year's Eve. And at midnight he would open a bottle of champagne and when all the glasses were filled, he would offer a toast: "To The United States of America." And the thought of this makes me choke up.

Maybe I'm part Italian. Anyway, I've learned there are some things that cannot be spoken out loud. I learned this from Pop. He always couched his deepest feelings in jest or gesture. All of us Barneses are feelers and touchers. More so than other families I've known. We touch one another and kiss a lot.

"Why not," Pop says, "we're animals, aren't we?"

And he's not even my real father. But I've been sitting up for four days, and when you're tired, your emotions are close to the surface. Still, it's a self-indulgence, I guess. To hell with it.

The bus churns on. Off to the left I can see the outline of the Green Mountains which are gray through the mist, and I think again about what I'm up to and why I'm going where I'm going, which is not directly home. But even that last observation is not exactly correct, because in a certain technical sense that is exactly where I'm going.

We are still an hour away from Burlington, Vermont, and the light is dimming and there is nothing to do but wait. And then my hat slides off the overhead rack and when I dust it off to put it back I come across Magruder's letter which is tucked in the sweatband and which

I have read only once since I first got it the day I left Kumi. It doesn't read as funny as it did the first time, but I guess it's my fatigue. All about the chow and the comings and goings in his bedpan battalion and the life in Saigon and the brutal silliness of it all. Finally he gets around to the reason for the letter, which is to tell me to keep open the month of April because he has it fixed up with Stanley Nelson and somebody he calls What-sername to take off for some spring skiing in Aspen and then do a run down the Green River with this friend of Stanley's who is a white-water expert. He says, ". . . so don't get married or go to jail or become a priest, at least until we've had a chance to slide down the Rockies and over the rapids."

The thing about the Gruder is that he is hard to be a big brother to. He is four years younger than me and yet he isn't. Or at least he hasn't been since we've grown up. Mostly I'm content to lie down with my feet in the air sipping beer and listening to pretty music; then along will come the Gruder with an idea about climbing a mountain or rowing to Long Island or taking a kayak trip down the Housatonic or some other nutty exercise, and I'm as apt as not to tag along. Not because I particularly enjoy discomfort, but because you never know how one of the Gruder's adventures is going to turn out. Like the scheme to row to Long Island. We were halfway across the Sound on this hot Fourth of July, Gruder, Stanley and me, blistered and sweaty and cussing the Gruder for getting us into the mess when along comes a big fat cabin cruiser out of Larchmont with a crew of three Sicilian sirens, who I thought might be the progeny of some Mafia biggies. Well, Magruder promotes our rowing excursion across Long Island Sound into a boozy weekend cruise to Block Island with lots of laughs and many interesting juxtapositions, and the Gruder inventing games and singing songs and generally turning on this little Sicilian pomidora who falls for him and starts crying in the wee hours and he turning the by now almost dreary scene by another surprise—quoting Dante and d'Annunzio and a lot of other Italian poets she was surprised to learn about just before she fell asleep in his arms. I never knew he knew the Italian poets existed much less was able to quote them from memory. This all happened after I realized that I had to stop hating the Gruder's guts. That I could no longer beat him and didn't have the energy to lead him so I might as well join him. Maturation it's called.

Chapter

Two

I have been in Burlington many times before, but always on Fridays about midnight en route to Stowe or Sugarbush. It looks different in daylight. Bleak. Sooty. Maybe shabby is the best word.

That pukey feeling is in my gut, sipping sweet coffee at the counter in the bus terminal. Too tired to eat. Too hungry to feel good. The homely countergirl stands, arms folded, by the icebox stealing sidelong glances in my direction. I guess she doesn't see many strangers dressed as I am. I look down at my Aussie hat on the counter. I made it one lonely evening sitting outside my hut in Kumi. It has a nice slice of leopard skin for a band. The flight bag I bought at the terminal in Nairobi. And a black tailor fashioned the bush jacket in a single afternoon sitting on the curb on the main drag of Entebbe.

Out in the street a chill fall wind is blowing the last yellow leaves from the elms in the green. Which way now? I know his name, but which way to find him? So I ask and am surprised how strange it is to be able to ask in my own language and get a reply in kind.

I find the place. This is where he is. This is the last leg. A stubby guy in a gold coat and crewcut approaches.

"Can I sell you a car today, sir?"

"No thanks," I say. "I just want to speak with Mr. Campbell," and turn to study the floor model, a pig painted baby-shit brown that Detroit proudly calls a "muscle car." I get in and slam the door and grab hold of the wheel. Sweat pours from my palms and smears. Then Campbell is standing beside the door and the pitch has begun. Trapped. But I will be kind—and patient. I will listen to the voice and study the face. Then I will say thank you and leave. That is, after all, the only reason I came here. To see Campbell for the first and last time and then leave.

Campbell has me out of the car. The hood raised. Talk about twin carbs and zero to sixty and the hood slams down and he asks for the order. I stare. Silence.

"I'm sorry, Mr. Campbell. I . . . I . . . I'm sorry to take up your time. But I don't want to buy the car."

"You don't want to buy the car?"

I look around the quiet showroom hoping that the crack in the floor will open and swallow me up.

As he starts to speak I interrupt, "No . . . see, you've got to understand. I came here to see *you*."

He just stares at me, ready for the pronouncement which follows.

"Mr. Campbell, . . . I'm your son."

He stares back at me steadily. Frozen. And I wish I'd kept my secret. But it's too late, and we can do naught but study each other and wonder.

Chapter

Three

It is near four o'clock when I get to the highway outside Burlington. A pickup driven by a Baptist preacher
takes me as far as Middlebury, where I must stand for
an hour dancing to keep warm before a big semi bears
down to a stop with electrically triggered pneumatic
belches. The cab door swings open and wailing soul
pours out. In the dim light of the dashboard I can see
the gleaming sweat of a black brow and the shine of a
white smile.

"Bridgeport?"

"Pretty close. I ain' spoda pick up no hitchers . . .
but you look okay."

Loud soul and shifting gears, and he reaches for the
radio knob, mercifully turning down the music.

"You don't look dressed very warm."

"Been overseas."

"You been in Vietnam?"

"Africa."

The black man looks off for a moment trying to figure how to field this one. Then smiling, "I never been in the old country."

I grin in reply, and the ice is broken.

"How long you over there?"

"Couple of years."

"You in the Peace Corps or somethin' like that?"

I nod.

"You trying to change the world or change your luck?"

I shrug it off with a grin.

And he comes back, "Well, you sho beat the draft!" laughing at his joke.

I agree. And again it's quiet except for the drone of the truck. He tunes in some gentle rock.

Going home. And all the thoughts that this brings forth.

I read somewhere once that you go back from whence you came for the same reasons you left in the first place. Of course, you're never quite sure of why you left in the first place.

At the time I signed up I thought I was leaving to defer the moment when the draft board would say, "I want you!" Then, too, there was the thing of wanting to do something different. After all, I figured I'd done all there was to do in Wilton, Connecticut, and figured I'd done all there was to be done and that could be done in college. I thought life had lost most of its mysteries. Of the few that remained the most intriguing and enigmatic was the self, and what better way to discover that than by getting out from under and setting yourself apart from those who love you too much and hover over you too much and generally try to keep you from growing the hell up. Yet I marvel at the power of the ties of home and relish the memory of old sounds and smells and feelings dredged up in recalling the little moments. I think again of how much life is coming and going, and remember the time when Mamma and Pop were going off to Europe leaving us with the sitter, Miss Putney. And how Nellie was screaming bloody murder as they pulled out of the driveway and Miss Putney started slapping her face when they were out of sight. I remember how the three of us, Nellie, Magruder and me, hid from her in the treehouse, and how this one day she came looking for us.

She stood below by the trunk of the oak peering up trying to catch a glimpse of us through the hole in the floor.

"Come down from there this minute. I know you're up there."

And then Magruder, who couldn't have been more than six or so, was struck by an incandescent idea. And while the harpie screamed and threatened below he carefully unzipped, arched his back, and forcing all the pressure he could muster sent a needle spray through the yawning hole. I was quick to join and cross his

stream, sending her screaming back to the house holding her wet red hair, her white uniform now dyed a subtle yellow, and Nell smiled and I danced a silent jig as
the Gruder zipped up. I paid for it. But it was worth it.

The lights of filling stations, farmhouses and villages
speed past and I look over to the driver who is yawning
and changing radio stations and downshifting on hills
and he yawns again and the world fades away to sleep,
and finally I'm standing on the edge of the Connecticut
Thruway at dawn and my semi is shifting and bellowing
and diminishing toward New York.

Chapter

Four

I must stand outside the house for a moment. In Africa I always pictured it in summer with everything green and the flag flying from the pole in the lawn, and the bright sunlight punctuating every tortured detail of this carpenter's fantasy in wood. Its builder must have had in mind a craftsman's monument to the family of Victorian times, with a big kitchen, a dining room and a couple of parlors with corner fireplaces finished in glazed green brick, and upstairs plenty of bedrooms for grandparents and mothers and fathers and children and even a room up the backstairs where a hired girl could sleep. And surrounding the whole structure a huge ring-around porch for wicker furniture and hooks for a swinging settee. So the man who built it did not just build a house. He built home. The absolute and total and final and definitive ultimate home.

Yet standing here in the early November sun and watching a light pop on in the kitchen window I see it as a strange place—somehow alien—because for now and forever I will be a guest in this house. That's not the way I want it, nor is it certainly the way they want it. That's just the way it has to be. For home is a home when it is sufficient—when it's a world unto itself, and there is plenty or more than plenty to enable and encourage and stimulate. And this passes and you leave. But coming back is a kind of quick replenishment and then it's time to go again. Coming and going. Being born and dying. Opening and closing doors. What happens in between is called living. And that's why I'm savoring the opening of this door yet again. And must go in now and take up quietly where I left off.

It's nearly time for breakfast, and I stand silently in the doorway to the kitchen and Mamma is prattling to Pop who has left the room and I don't want to interrupt. But I want to touch her. I want to hug her. And hold her. And smell her clean smell. And press my lips to her soft cheek and somehow tell her how much—how much— And she prattles on . . .

"Mamma—" and she doesn't hear.

"Mamma—I've missed you, Mamma."

And I step into the room as she stops talking, seeing that she is unwilling to turn and risk the shattering of her hopes. But I'm behind her now and she does turn and I touch her and hug her and hold her and smell her clean smell and press my lips to her soft cheek and cry because somehow I can't tell her how much—

"George—George, come here. Sam—Sam—" She is crying, too.

"Why didn't you tell us?"

Now Pop has taken over. He kisses me and I feel his strong grip on the back of my neck and the three of us are standing there in the kitchen wondering and embarrassed and looking for the thread to start again.

"You son of a bitch—you didn't call," says Pop, bringing the scene back into focus.

"Saved a nickel."

"Yes, but you scared your poor mother half out of her wits. We could have met you at the airport."

"Where's Nellie?" I ask.

And Mamma asks, "Sam, have you had breakfast? You must be starved."

"Your sister's asleep," Pop says. "She's been running around with a lawyer. Chases ambulances by day and your sister by night."

As he walks me to the hall, Mamma says, "Go get her up while I get you some breakfast."

Pop follows me to the stairs. "Whole generation going to hell in a hand-basket. She should be married to some nice, kindly, advertising man and raising little account executives." Then, as I'm halfway up the stairs he looks up. "Sam . . . I'm glad you're back."

"Same here, Pop." I look back at his craggy old face for just a trifle too long and have to get the hell out of sight.

No answer when I knock on her door. So I open it quietly. The drawn shade is blowing softly and when my eyes adjust to the darkness I see Nell asleep, her hair tossed carelessly on the pillow. The framed picture of the Everly Brothers is gone from her dresser and in its place is a shot of me standing barechested against the African sky. Beside it is a big picture of Magruder in his uniform. Otherwise it's Nellie's room as it always was—not messy, but careless. Clothes dropped here and there, and a pink slip hanging from the bedpost.

She stirs as I sit on the edge of her bed, and I study that sweet face. She's a woman now. Old enough to vote, and yet the elfin innocence has not left her.

Softly, I say, "Nell—Nellie," and see a slight nod of annoyance. So I bend an old Milne poem: " 'Wetherbee George Dupree took great care of his sister, although he was only three.' Sam, Sam, said to his sister," and she bolts upright and hugs me. " 'Sister, he said, said he, you must never go down to the end of the town without consulting me.' " And all the while she is hugging me and saying, "Sam, Sam, Sam."

"Hi, Sis."

"You're skinny," she says, holding me by the shoulders, those big fawnlike saucers darting over my face. "You're positively a skeleton."

"Who is the lawyer?"

"A friend. Just a buddy."

That's good, I muse. A put-down.

"Sammy, Sammy. I want to hear all about it. Tell me everything. Why are you so late? When did you get in?

You were supposed to get here ages ago. Mummy thought you were going to be here Monday. And when you didn't show or we didn't hear, we thought you'd been eaten by cannibals."

That was Nell. Questions and declarations, and a pause to smile and look. "How dare you break into my room without knocking? What will the neighbors say? You've changed, Sammy."

"You, too."

She was pleased. "Have I, Sam? . . . how?"

"Big boobs."

"You're obscene."

I agree and stand to look at her twitching my nose and realizing I don't smell too good.

"Showertime. Come on, Nell. Grab your socks. I'll see you downstairs."

As I move toward the door and take the doorknob in hand, I have an idea and turn to her. "I stopped by Burlington." She doesn't get it. "I saw the old man." She gets it and gasps.

"Oh, Sam!—Tell me!"

"It will keep," I say and I leave.

Chapter

Five

Soap and hot water. Good, like I remembered it. The john is filled with steam as I rub my frame dry with a clean white towel, then note the incongruity of Mamma's froufrou initials embroidered on it as I go over my hairy legs. The door opens and Pop walks in carrying a can of beer. He puts the lid of the pot down, sits, and hands me the beer.

"The honeymoon is over." Pop likes old jokes and old friends.

He looks me over as I begin to shave. I pause and take a swig. The beer is cold and good, and I get off a nice burp.

He's looking me over and must be wondering how to start.

"You look skinny. Get sick over there?"

"Nope."

"Malaria? Any of that stuff?"

"Nope. I stayed pretty well on a diet of camel liver and cassava."

"Probably brought back a good dose."

And noting where he is sitting I say, "In that case you better find another chair." I swig some beer from the can, watching him over the edge as I drink. "Hey, . . ." I say in my best could-care-less manner, ". . . are we getting us a lawyer in the family?"

He looks up and away for a second and thrusting out his lower lip, he points down with his thumb.

"Is it that bad?"

"Oh, I don't know. Nell's got some kind of thing about him. But it just seems the more she sees him the unhappier she gets." He looks away now and I shave on. "Maybe it's dumb of me to want so much for my kids." Then looking back at me and leaning on the bowl where my beer is resting, he says, "What do *you* want, Sam?"

"I want you to quit blocking my beer," nudging him out of the way.

"Well, you know how women are," Pop says, now shifting to neutral ground, and pointing to his head.

"Pop . . . she just thinks she's screwed up."

I have to muse about whether to tell him where I've been and who I've seen. But I figure why keep secrets. After all, we're two grown men. My mouth is suddenly dry and I wet it from the can. Pop discovers a new fascination with his shoe.

"Pop . . . you never knew my real father?"

He takes it head on. "All I knew about him was that he was of sound mind and body . . . and unlike me he was fertile . . . at the time of your conception."

I shave. I shave and wonder how I'm going to frame it and how it will sound when I do.

"I went to see him." My father for just a second starts to look up and away from his shoe, then quickly returns.

"I found his name quite by accident. In my Peace Corps health file. A bureaucratic accident. And traced it down as soon as I landed." Another sip of brew. "Went to see him."

And there is this long pause which neither of us can do anything about. I felt the need to tell it, and Pop must understand a territory where the footing is dangerous. But he will think of something. He will think of something, because I can't.

"I just can't imagine life without you kids—you and Nell. And ole Magruder . . . Hey . . . we just got a letter from Magruder." He fishes it out of a back pocket and dons his specs. "Here . . . I'll read it." And he scans it for a second and as we move out of the john and into the bedroom he begins.

As he finishes the letter, I'm sitting on the bed in my shorts putting on some clean socks. I'm indignant. "Why did he go?"

"Where?" Pop says.

"Into service."

"What the hell kind of a question is that? He got a little letter that said, 'Greetings.' "

"I didn't, and don't tell me Magruder's a hawk, or that he thinks the Viet Cong are going to go marching up Sunset Boulevard."

"You can't figure that out? You really can't?"

I can only shake my head and wait.

"Well, he gave every reason but the real one. And I don't think he knows the real one. He let himself be drafted because his big brother didn't. He wanted to do it different."

I'm listening, and comprehending, but not understanding. Perhaps I'm afraid to. Pop goes on.

"Not better—or more noble—but just different. Different from you."

"You mean he was sore because I didn't go?"

"No, not at all. Just looking for a different bag as they say."

"What a bag," I say as I thrash in the closet for something clean to wear. Magruder, I can see, was buying his clothes in the Mod Department of Bloomingdale's. He'd do it for laughs.

"Hurry down, Sam. Your breakfast is waiting," Pop says as he leaves.

Alone in the room that was mine and Magruder's, I find a funny-looking shirt and a pair of pants whose designer must have been intent on bringing back the codpiece.

SOCCER POWER! reads a sign on the mirror. And under

it a group shot of preppies in soccer uniforms. Captain Magruder Barnes is all smiles seated in the middle flanked by teammates. He looks like Mamma. I must look like mine.

I'd seen movies of DiMaggio once. He turned and ran for a ball that Greenberg had hit toward deep right. I held my breath as he took those great strides. The grace and fluid motion. Like a deer. The stunning leap, arm outstretched. No motion wasted as he pulled it down and threw it in. That's the way Magruder runs. Like DiMaggio. Easy. Like he's always running downhill. Or like he was on a trampoline in slow motion. But he can be a pain in the ass. Especially when Nellie is around. Little brothers are a pain in the ass. But if you have to have one, I'll take the Gruder.

Now I'm standing in the doorway of the kitchen again and they are together, Mamma staring in dismay at my costume. Then Pop, who's been reading the *Times*, looks up, and his jaw drops.

"Oh, God. Not another one!"

"Wait 'til you see me in long hair," I say, noting that Nell is enjoying the put-on.

"Did you ever smoke pot?" Pop asks.

I shrug and ignore it. I really want to ask him if he ever played with himself, or drank bathtub gin. Instead I say, "Mamma, I'm a new man."

"It's outa sight," Nell chirps.

But Mamma has her worried expression. "I think you've lost weight. I think you should go straight to Dr. Robinson and get a complete checkup."

Nell has a better idea. "I think he should put the money into meat and potatoes."

"Right, Sis," I say. "Come on, kid. Let's go picket the Pentagon."

Mamma has laid on sausages and flapjacks with maple syrup and takes pleasure in the way I cut into them.

"Did Gruder wear this stuff out on the street?" I ask. "I mean like every day?"

"Sure," says Nell, "right up to the day he marched off to war."

I look at Mamma whose worry has not left. "I look good, Mamma. This is the new me."

"Oh, Sam. I hope you're not serious. I hope you're teasing . . . Sam . . ."

I've gone too far. "Now Mamma——" But it's too late. She's off.

"But, Sam. If you're going back to the wire service, they will expect some——"

I have to cut her off. "Wire service. Mamma, I'm back five minutes, and already you're blocking out my career. I don't know what I'm going to do. Maybe back to the old job. Maybe not. Maybe I'll open a nightclub, or become a pool shark. I just don't know." The heat has built up too high and I pause and, in a quieter tone, I say, "I'm twenty-three years old."

"And in seven short years you will be over thirty and old enough to be excluded from the mainstream of American society as we are," Pop concludes testily.

"Sam is only joking," Nell says as she tries to save the day.

But I won't let her. "No, I'm not. I'm twenty-three, and since age twenty-one I have considered myself a guest in this house. I love you all, but let's face it, the time is long since gone when you could or should fuss over how I'm going to lead my life." Not wanting to survey the damage about me, I pick up the last morsel of pancake.

"Whew!" Nell says, "I guess that puts us in our place."

She still doesn't get it, so I tell her quietly: "And maybe it's time you broke your plate, too, Nell."

I feel Mamma's hand grip my shoulder. Strongly. "Sam, there are times when you are lacking in feeling. Now, for instance."

Pop stands and says quietly, "We've got a cord of wood to chop out back. Get the ax and work off some of that bile."

Chapter

Six

There's a big rock out on the hill in back of the house. It's impacted with mica and rough garnets. We used to take a knife and pry them loose dreaming of riches. One day we even took a handful down to Mr. Haley who owns the jewelry store. But he was busy and ran us out. I am sitting on the rock now. I'm more comfortable in blue jeans and a lumber shirt after that outfit of Magruder's. I can see the house below, partly hidden behind the oak, and the weathered outline of the tree-house. Surprised that Pop hasn't knocked it down after all these years. Maybe he's saving it for grandchildren, I muse. It's November, and there's a sting in the wind that blows that fluid, red grass that grows in abundance in these idle fields in Connecticut.

I wait here because I know she's coming. I don't know when. But she will come. Because she will want to find out. But then, again, maybe she really couldn't care less. That's one of the differences between the Gruder and Nell. She's contrary. She's got a personality like a ball with backspin. You see it flying through the air in one direction and when it hits the ground it backs up. The other thing about Nell is that she is not a thoroughly modern female. She is part Victorian and part libertarian and the Victorian part of her is the scared part and the libertarian part of her is where she is headed if she can stop being scared shitless of what people will think and stop worrying over whether or not she might hurt somebody's feelings. Like not being able to turn down an invitation to a marshmallow roast on a rainy night or spending three days looking for a laundry ticket because the laundry man might scold her for the inconvenience. But the libertarian part I'm sure about because that's the way she is when she's around the Gruder and me. At these times her ass swings free, and she laughs out loud and whistles like a sergeant and swears good and is never shocked by our gamy banter. She comes on strong with what she thinks is good and bad and gets mad and lets it all hang out.

And this is a far different Nellie than the one the outside world sees. When I was still at Bowdoin and she was at Smith, I used to fix her up with dates on house-party weekends. The first time was her freshman year, and it was disaster. I paired her off with a nice, dumb, quiet halfback and he got bombed on three beers and ripped her blouse and sent her screaming back to the chem prof's house where she was staying. So I got smarter the next time and lined her up with a gentle Irish guy from Nashua, New Hampshire, who was headed for the priesthood. This seemed to work out all right. They would always stay close to bright lights, and she could do her guitar-sing thing which made him proud, and they could always rap about Thomas Aquinas or Marsilio of Padua and dance around quietly, with Nell always looking over his shoulder to see if I was still there. Of course, she'd get nervous if I disappeared for any length of time, and this sort of cramped my yearnings because I had a thing going at this time with a girl named Gloria which did not square with the presence of a whimpering kid sister.

Everybody thinks that January is the beginning. Not me. For me the beginning is the fall of the year. First day of school. New teachers. New schools. Good-bye to summer days and old leaves. Hello to winter snows. Sad somehow and scary. And I think again how much of life is coming and going. Hello and good-bye. And being alone.

I wish she would hurry up. I am ready to split when I see old Pot Luck cutting across the lower field by the brook. Nell's pigtails flying as she hangs on with bare thighs. God, can she ride.

She knows I'm watching. Now taking the stone wall, leaning forward, then straight back. A sharp whack on the horse's ass and he steams up the hill. She reins him sharply and cuts across the field by the reservoir. Then she pulls him in and he snorts and pants, and she smiles down from her nervous perch. We stare each other out, and I'm enjoying the game. I don't budge.

Finally she asks, "Guru . . . Oh, Guru . . . what is the secret of life?"

So I tell her, "The secret of life? The secret of life, my child, is a good roll in the hay." She should have known better than to ask. "Hey, Nell . . . are you still a virgin?" I no sooner get the words out, than I'm thinking what a dumbshit question it was.

I wish I could erase it. But I know you can't erase or unsay or unpunch or unfart. Once it's said, it's said. It's spoken and heard and on the record and you have to live with it.

She slides down off the bare back, comes around to take off the bridle, and then slaps his ass and watches him take off for the barn. Then she looks at me, both saucers boring in. She nods a little nod, still staring, and then says, "I want you to tell me everything."

I've always liked the part where she wants me to give her something. I like to hold back and watch the frustration. Watch her plead and cajole, taunt and threaten. I like to play wise and knowing and unreachable, watching her fever rise—for half a Popsicle when we were kids or for secrets and gossip now that we've grown.

"Nah . . . you don't want to hear it, Sis."

She's beside me on the rock; her hands clutch my shirt, and she's shaking me.

"But I do, Sam . . . I do . . . Sam, please."

And then I realize I don't really want to tell the story.

I don't want to reach for the words and sort out the sequence and live it over again because it was nothing. Once it was over, it was nothing. So to hell with it.

"Tell you what I'm going to do . . . just for you. Now I wouldn't do this for just any broad . . . but because you're a poisonal friend of mine, . . . and you are my kin . . . though no blood relative . . . and in spite of the fact that you're my rival sibling . . . I'm gonna spill out the whole seamy saga . . . right here before your very eyes . . . that is on one small condition."

She sees a trap. Her guard is up. "What's that?"

I explain that I want her to tell me what she thinks it was like. Sort of like show me yours first, and then I'll show you mine. And I also suspect that she's lived the thing out in fantasy many times before, and I am curious to discover how similar to mine her anxieties have been about this.

She just sits there, head down and shaking her head no. And finally, "Oh, Sam, I just couldn't. I couldn't."

"The deal's off."

"That's dirty. That's not fair."

"It was John F. Kennedy who said, 'Life is not fair.' "

Now she's looking off and mulling over the deal. "I may say something to hurt, Sam."

"No way."

And thinking for a while, looking this way and that, but not at me. "Sam, why are you making me do this?"

I can only shrug and wonder why she is wearing pigtails and no bra and what she is like. Really like, to someone who is not her brother.

Then taking a deep breath she ventures, "Well . . . first, you went to the agency . . ." And now looking at me, "Oh, Sam, I can't . . . I can't . . . it's too spooky."

"Go. Go. Go. Good therapy."

"Must I?"

I nod.

"But you mustn't look. It's too awful . . ."

"Let's walk then." And, as she talks fast, we walk slowly into the November wind.

"So you went up to the agency, and there's a big brass knob on an iron door. You go in. It's quiet. You hear your feet clicking on the marble floor. And there is a reception desk. And behind the desk is a kindly old lady who says, 'What do you want?' And you say, 'I'm Sam Barnes, and I'm now of age, and could I now see the file on my adoption history?' She scurries away to go tell Mrs. Big. And you stand there first on one foot and then the other. And she scurries back to tell you now you can see Mrs. Big. Mrs. Big is an ogre. The wicked witch. She wants you to go away. But she can't make you do that because you are Sam Barnes. And so she pushes a button and the kindly old lady puts you in an oak-paneled room with a file."

We are in the stand of pines by the reservoir now. I'm leaning against a tree, and Nell, her back to me, is standing apart telling it. I hear a quiver in her voice, and her head goes down.

". . . a red cardboard file with a black ribbon . . . you untie . . . I . . . I can't go on . . ." She is almost sobbing. "I can't Sam, I can't."

I go over to her and turn her to me. Her eyes are wet, and her expression torn.

"You were doing so well." But I look closer. "You're really scared."

Again I'd like to erase and start again, and unsay and undo. But I can only try to repair. So I tell it.

"Well, you were wrong about going to the agency. They would never—legally they can't let us see the records. At least not without a court order. And that's nigh impossible to come by. No, I found out by sheer, blind luck. A slip of paper in my Peace Corps records, but to hell with that part of it, Nell. It turns out he's a car dealer in Burlington. I never meant to let on who I was. I was ready to call it quits and get out of there. I don't know why, but I couldn't. I somehow couldn't leave without laying it out. So I just said, 'Mr. Campbell, I'm your son. My name is Sam Barnes.' And we stood there for ten years just staring at each other. Everything quiet except a typewriter in the distance. He looked at me like it was some kind of a sick prank, which maybe it was, and he finally said, 'What did you say your name was?' So I told him again and tried to explain that I didn't want anything and just wanted to say hello and then go away and never come back. He seemed to accept this and took me into his glass cage and lit a smoke and let it roll out of his mouth, all the time looking at me. Then he told me I caught him by surprise, and I apologized. And I told him I don't know what got into me, and then I tried to explain about adopted kids, and some of the hangups they're apt to have when they reach a certain age. And all the while I kept getting up to leave, and he kept asking me to sit. Wanted to know am I all right, and about Africa, and wanted to know about Mamma and Pop and how we lived . . . and all the while he kept looking at me. I don't think I look that much like him. And finally I tightened my gut and asked about the mother of the child, and just as he was about to handle that bomb this kid bursts into the office and says, 'Hey, Pop, can I have the keys to the Chevy?' And the old man tossed them to him, and he walked off. I watched my half brother pick up something and go out the front door, and when I looked back he was in one of his stares, and then he looked up and asked if there was anything he could give me. I asked again about my mother, but he just looked away. So I got up to go and offered him my hand, which he didn't notice. He just said, 'I loved her. That's all I can give you.' And so we shook and I left him standing in the cage and made my way past the floor models toward the door at the other end and went by the lady typing at the desk to the door and then opened it. She didn't look up as I passed so I closed it and went back to ask her the time. She told me, but I wasn't listening. I just searched that face, taking too long to do it, and then split."

Chapter

Seven

My arm is around Nell's back now, and we are coming across the back lawn. We haven't said anything in the walk home. When we're alone, Nell and I, we don't talk much. Usually. I like it better, and perhaps she does, too, because talk spoils a special way of feeling, and at these times she has a distant way of looking and acting. How can I explain it? When we're alone and we don't talk. There is this special mood that takes over as if Nellie were not my sister but someone else.

Now we're under the oak. I look up and there it is. There is a rotten timber in the floor, and most of the slats are missing in the sides. I can see daylight through the roof, and a last, weathered strand of the rope ladder is blowing out in the wind.

"Happy days," I say. "Pop ought to tear it down."

"Oh, no! If I had my way, we'd fix it up and live in it."

"Oh, come off it, Sis," I say, surprised at my impatience. Then out of nowhere I hear myself saying, "How do you know you love the guy?"

"What makes you so sure I do?"

"I'm not saying you do or don't. I haven't even met him."

"Well, you will. He's picking me up tomorrow and we're off to Vermont."

Nell is too young to be running off with some meatball on a ski weekend, and I don't know why the old folks let her, especially if they don't like him.

"Well, don't break a leg." And just so my real concern is not lost, I add, "And remember, they haven't perfected the cherry transplant."

Chapter

Eight

There is nothing like a sharp ax against dry wood. I sharpened it myself in the woodshed on the old whet-stone. Swinging an ax is good because you see the results right away. A good, clean chop makes a nice sound, too. Besides, a lot of good things come out of chopping. You get firewood. Exercise. Plenty of action before your eyes. And if you're angry, you can let it out. Or if you happen to have an audience, you get respect. They have wood-chopping contests up in Canada, don't they? So all my wood-chopping plans for the day are made to co-incide with the arrival of Justin Clarke, who is a meat-ball. This I realize is an *a priori* judgment, but piss on him.

All during breakfast Mamma has been clucking about

the roads, and if this young man is a careful driver, and really Nellie, you should both stay here tonight and get a good start tomorrow when there's less traffic, and you will both be rested. But Nell is getting antsy and saying the plans are already made and Justin's an excellent driver, and please don't interfere, after all she's twenty-one and can take care . . . and on and on.

So after lunch I saunter out the back door wearing my Paul Bunyan shirt. It's cold, so naturally I have on shorts made of cut-down Levis which not only show off my hairy legs, but also demonstrate how oblivious I am to pain and cold.

I check the ax head again for nicks, hoping to delay the performance 'til the audience shows up. It's clean and shiny and ready, so there is no longer any *real reason* to wait, and then I realize what a bratty, baby, churlish, sorehead, adolescent thing I'm into. So I put a big log on the block and *Pow!* Mad. Goddamn mad! Not at the meatball. At Sam. Grow up, Goddammit. *Pow!* And the logs are splitting clean and flying all over the yard. And pretty soon I hear the fart of a snotty foreign sportscar downshifting and turning into the driveway, burning rubber to a stop. The slam of a door and then silence.

I chop on, but it isn't the way I thought it would be.

I know they are watching from the window. I thought Nell would bring him out to meet me before this. Chop on, chop on, oh, mighty woodsman. And I think maybe she's so sore about what she thinks I think of him that maybe she will leave without introducing us. So maybe I should give up and go in. And I come down with a *Thwonk* that sinks the head two inches into the block and sends a log flying across the lawn to land at the dancing feet of Justin Clarke, Nell not far behind. I win.

Class. Not the Magruder kind of class that seems to derive from some special grace the Lord bestows for reasons of His own. But the class that is bred when money marries money. It's a mannered charm. A set of learned reflexes that go with country club, private school, Brooks Brothers clothes, and a staff in the kitchen. Even the accent is part of the reflex. I don't mean to say that it's good or bad. I only mean to say that it is. It's there. A lot of guys at school tried to fake it, and that was sickening. But Justin Clarke is not faking it. It's real. It's him. It's all he knows. If he's a meatball, it's not for this reason. Rather, it's because he is a meatball. Period.

And now we are talking about ten inches of new powder at Mad River, and no, I can't join them because I've got to get to the city to seek my fortune, and he's looking up at the treehouse and wondering. I explain how it was a sanctuary when we were kids, and Nell mentions how I just got back from Africa, by which time we have walked back into the kitchen, and he's telling the assembled about the time his dad took his family to Kenya on a safari years ago. Mamma offers him some milk for his tea, but he says he takes only lemon, which she slices up and sets before him, as he lights up a little cigar and proceeds to tell us all about Africa, Nell passing through carrying her luggage and packing it into the car, and loading her skis and coming back into the house to fetch Justin Meatball.

The scene has played ten minutes. He does stop the monologue at one time to inquire where I served, and while I know it's always awkward standing around making small talk with the relatives of a girl you're shacking up with, I suppose I should make allowances. And I'm ready to do it, right up until they are standing ready to leave, when he snuffs out his cigarillo in Mamma's untouched lemon slices and he starts to lay on those North Shore lockjaw phrases like "Awfully nice" and "Really marvelous" and they're out the door and off. Up his.

Chapter

Nine

As I step out the back door, Pop is backing the Green Debris out of the barn. He has two cars, the Blue Debris, which is the one Mamma drives, and the Green Debris, which is his station car. He bought them both years ago in a fit of pique and rebellion at the Detroit people. I think these two cars were probably the last two built in South Bend, Indiana. But he likes them because they are the only cars made then and since designed to accommodate the human head with hat and also the windows therein were put there for looking out of and the doors are big enough so you don't have to crawl in and out on your hands and knees. So he found a guy in the village who, over the years, could keep them running in good shape, although this did require main-

taining a vigorous correspondence with the parts people
in South Bend and keeping a continual surveillance of
new arrivals at the auto junkyards in Norwalk. Pop
didn't do this because he was a tightwad, but simply because he liked the two cars better than anything that
was currently being sold. The Gruder used to try to talk
him into new models and once even got him into a
showroom, but when Pop was getting into a fat, potbel-
lied tube-shaped car it knocked his hat off, and he mut-
tered something about not wanting to own a mecha-
nized beer barrel and stomped off in a huff. So, soon
after that the Gruder dubbed the cars the Blue and the
Green Debris and, since then, we've learned to love
them as Pop does.

The house is in Wilton, but Pop takes the train from
Darien. And if you're out of the driveway at seven
twenty-six you have no trouble parking, buying a paper,
and catching the seven fifty-seven. Darien is where the
hard-nosed, dedicated, meat-eating commuters live.
That's not quite right. That's where their families live,
and where they keep their boats and buy their liquor,
and where they sleep when the trains are running. Otherwise the commuters live on the stalled railroad cars, in
the offices, gin mills, taxis, clubs, and apartments of
secretaries in the city.

We are on the road by seven twenty-six and Pop is re-
laxed. No sweat. We'll make the train. He's muttering
about the SST and the waste of it all. "Hell," he says,
"this is the age of the railroad, not the high-speed plane.

We have no problem getting to Paris. We have a problem getting to work!"

I'm smiling at him and how sore he is at the President. But he voted for him and got what he voted for.

He parks the car, and we climb the knoll to the platform, an act which Pop seems to do automatically, and walk briskly toward the station, passing the commuters standing alone and by twos, holding their folded *Times* and peering up the tracks. Pop says hello to Mr. Howe and the headhunter, Mr. Fleming. Then he nods at a few others along the way.

Commuters don't talk. That's bad form. Mostly they leave each other alone. They give each other as much room as possible before the city closes in on them.

I follow Pop into the station and stand in the fast-moving line to buy his *Times* and then we're out on the platform again, and some guy has quietly asked him if he will be in the office this morning because he wants to chat about something or other. Pop says he will be. Commuters, especially, don't talk business at the station. That's the worst form. I don't know who wrote the rules.

As the man walks off, Pop whispers, "Watch out." I turn around in time to see Mr. Nelson bearing down on us, but it's too late for a getaway.

Mr. Stanley Nelson is a runty guy who married an Amazon and in a remarkable juxtaposition of genes begat Stanley Junior, who stands six five and is Magruder's best friend. We used to have pickup games when the reservoir was frozen over during Christmas vacations. He could skate and could check hard, but you could fake him easy. I always thought he was sort of yellow, but I never said this to the Gruder.

"Morning, George . . . eight minutes late out of Bridgeport. Nice day. A little damp." He looks at the sky. Hasn't seen me yet. Good. "Stanley called last night. Doing great . . . Captain of hockey, you know . . ."

And he goes on about how Stanley scored three times in a game last night and how he was burning the old midnight oil and getting the old marks and about how he wouldn't be surprised if Stan made cum laude. I'm ashamed to think how grossly I misjudged this friend of my brother's, and then he sees me.

"Oh, hello, Sam. Didn't notice you there. Haven't seen you around much lately. Been away or something?"

"Africa."

"Oh. A little vacation trip before stepping into the old man's shoes?"

"Peace Corps."

To make up for what I was thinking about Junior, I ask, "Stan up at Yale now?"

"Stanley? . . ." He looks away for a second and then turns back, "Hell no. He's at Vassar!" And he moves off to put himself on a collision course with the President of Abercrombie & Fitch.

Pop is smiling when I look back and says, "You coming home tonight or are you going to stay at Max's?"

"I'll play it by ear."

"I've got a bridge game with some boys in the last car. If you need help getting lined up, give me a call." He walks toward the end of the platform as the train groans in.

The commuting life holds no surprises for me. It's the norm. Pop has been doing it for all of his business life. I have neither accepted it nor rejected it for my own life-style. I never even thought about it. But on this November morning it takes on a new meaning.

I walk into the car and sit in the first empty seat by a window. The shady side. The car is half full, and I'm struck by the setting. A tableau. Each commuter sitting primly with the *Times* neatly folded down the middle, so it won't press against the guy in the next seat. Then in the middle of the car, on the sunny side, two seats facing each other, a hippie family. Him with a beard, beads, headband, and leather jacket, and her with a baggy gown, long tresses, and screaming baby. Another kid is squirming in the opposite seat. I think about that shot of the earth that they took from the moon, and the feeling that we're all riding this thing together.

As the train is grinding toward Noroton Heights, the conductor priest passes through punching tickets and offering the sacraments. Noroton Heights is a suburb of Darien. I have just made a funny joke. Among the natives it's referred to as Neurotic Heights.

And I'm sitting here beside the window, watching the steam surround the boarding passengers, anxious to get the show on the road.

The Norotoners are filing in, eyeing their seats as they

enter, and I recall the feeling that boarding passengers are intruders, until they get settled down, and how this probably has something to do with the territorial imperative. Then I notice that someone is standing in the aisle beside my seat.

I look up, but I don't know him and look back out the window. We are in motion now. And I hear, "Ahem." And I look back and he's still there staring at me, so I figure I must know him and smile. But he doesn't smile back, and my fly isn't open so I don't know what the hell's up. I try to look away, but again there's this anxious hovering. So I look at him giving him my most inquisitive expression.

Now the hippie baby is crying louder and louder. I look around to try to figure out why in hell he is hanging in. There are still plenty of empty seats.

I can see the poor guy is close to tears. I'm in a cold sweat and embarrassed and pretty sore, but who needs this? So I get up, and he slides in and I notice that all the newspapers have been lowered, and all eyes are on Sam Barnes. And I'm walking toward the rear of the car, and my eyes fall on that hippie family. Friends. So I take the seat facing the father, look, and flash him the "V."

"Peace."

"That scene was outa sight."

I shrug and notice the little ones eyeing me. The girl has her hands full with the screamer. And the rest of the passengers watch in dismay as the screaming goes on. Up theirs. She just can't cool him off, and I think maybe it's me, but then I had luck with babies in Uganda, and this one can't be that much different. So I say, "Let me try."

She's tired and glad to get rid of him and doesn't protest too much. And I'm glad to be able to cuddle the little critter. I don't know why. I guess it's that animal thing Pop talks about. So I squeeze it, and it stares back whimpering and catching its breath. When I look up again, some of the passengers are still peering. I return their stares in kind.

I didn't catch his last name. Some big, long Armenian jawbreaker, but his first name is Vic. If his bearded face is fierce, his voice is gentle. Without conceit or pretense. Because I knew he didn't, I ask, "You take this train every day?"

"Man, you blown your mind?" taking his wife's hand. "How come you have a way with kids?"

"I used to be a baby myself."

"How about you?" he asks. "You ride this thing every day?"

"First day. Maybe my last. I gotta find a job in the city. Any ideas?"

It was meant to be just another throwaway, but the comeback is quick.

"Sure. Go see my old man. If you want the establishment bit. He's President and Board Chairman of Great Eastern Industries and all its divisions and subsidiaries, Amen."

I must look stupid because he continues, "I'm serious . . . if that's your bag."

"I appreciate it."

The trip goes fast because his old lady just got back from a cane-cutting expedition to Cuba and he is telling all about that scene and what is happening with the New Left and how he dropped out and what it is like in the East Village. He talks a little about the dope world, and then, when I explain my Peace Corps thing they look at me like I'd been recruited by Warren Gamaliel Harding. The train is rattling across the Harlem River Bridge, and I'm looking down on what we've come to call the black ghetto. I have seen it before from the train. But I've just come from Africa, having seen the slums of Accra and Dakar and Cairo. For sheer disgust Harlem wins. And then the train carrying me and the President of Abercrombie & Fitch goes into the tunnel leading to Grand Central.

I help Vic and company take their gear off the train and then snag a luggage wagon to send them on their way, and they both say some nice things to me and we split. The livestock is riding the escalators into the Pan Am Building, I with them, and walking through I think that the mausoleum at Luxor must have scaled out about like this.

The satchel I'm carrying isn't that light, and I'm grateful for the good luck of nailing a cab. But by the time I reach down to pick up the satchel, get it poised and ready to toss into the back of the cab, some Mod-dressed creep and his moll get in, slam the door out of my hand, and the cab is off. Him grinning at me out of

the back window, flashing a smile of mah-jongg teeth.
I'm home.

To hell with it. I'll walk. But by the time I pass the
Waldorf, my arms are aching. Somewhere in Tennyson
there's a line about Ulysses, about being ". . . a part of
all that I have met." I have been in Africa, and it is part
of me now. So I put the bag on my head, holding on
with one hand on the handle, rep tie blowing in the
breeze, and hike to Max's studio on Central Park South.

Max is a friend. I worked as his assistant the summer
vacation before I quit Bowdoin. I'd just got home from
Maine and was wondering what to do for that summer
and our neighbors, the Benjamins, were over at the
house for dinner and I was showing off a second-hand
Nikon that I just bought, and Mr. Benjamin got to talking with me about photography and all. He had something to do with the ad business and happened to mention this guy he knew in the city who was a hotshot
photographer who needed an assistant and asked if I
wanted to talk with him. So I spent that summer cleaning up the studio, working in the darkroom on the black
and white stuff, carrying equipment on location, main-
taining all the gear in tip-top shape, and watching Max
make it happen.

Max is an original. I don't know how old he is. He is
no age. Maybe forty or fifty, but I never asked him. I
think he is as old as those who happen to be around
him. And most of the people who happen to be around
him are young, modelly chicks. While he has a wife and

a couple of teenage kids and is devoted to them, still, as I say, he seems to take on the same age as those about him and so he often has these little things on the side which I think derive from the intensity with which he goes about his thing, which, of course, is immortalizing in still pictures the most beautiful women in the world. But he loves to laugh and drink and eat Jewish food and go places and shoot pictures and see his work published in the chichi magazines and compare himself with the other types in that narrow world.

That summer if I'd goof and forget a lens or prop on location, or fail to give a call, or spoil a negative in the darkroom, or trip over the light wires in the studio he'd never get sore. He'd just figure out some imaginative way of turning the disaster into a creative triumph. He used to tease me, saying that with me as his assistant he could become better than Avedon. This was a kind way of telling me off, I guess. It pained me to goof when Max was hustling, so gradually I got better at the assistant's job and our friendship took on more balance and equality. And it pleased me to be friends with Max.

When I walk in, Max is shooting a chichi model in a setting of tinfoil and neon tubes. He's busy and doesn't notice my entrance. The strobes are flashing, the rock playing, the chick is bending this way and that, and Max is snapping away with his Hasselblad, all the time shouting and pleading and cajoling. Finally he pats her on the ass, tells her how great she is, and sends her off to the dressing room to change. Then he sees me.

"Sammy, Sammy! You're back!"

And he gives me a big hug and goes on about how he liked my postcards, and asking how were the broads, and saying how I've gotten skinny and then I fall for one of Max's pranks, which is when he asks to take your coat and he grabs it and throws it on the floor.

"You don't get any smarter, Sammy."

I laugh and pick it up. He sends Marty, his new assistant, out for coffee, and we sit and rap about what I'm going to do and how he was thinking of me just the other day because somebody from a weekly wanted a man to cover a job in Caracas that would be just right for me. He says that I should stay as long as I want right here in the studio because he has to go to Dallas ("Dallas, ugh") for a while; and no, I won't be any bother and the place is mine for as long as I need it and to help myself to the gefilte fish in the icebox and then he asks me about what I'm going to do now that I'm back and unemployed. I explain the idea I had coming through Harlem on the train and he winces.

"Shoot what? A slum? Sammy, it's been done to death. It'll never sell. People are tired of ugly."

"I'm tired of ugly."

"Then don't shoot ugly. Shoot pretty girls."

"I've done that. Besides . . . there's a way. There's a way to shoot ugly and make people feel it. Make 'em want to fix ugly and make ugly beautiful."

He goes on about what am I going to do for bread in the meantime, and says I got a talent. "Class," he calls it. But he goes along with my idea and agrees to lend me a couple of cameras and whatever else I need.

So I toss the suitcase on a packing crate and take out an old pair of khakis, my lumber shirt, and a pair of tennis shoes.

Max is amused. "You got a lovely wardrobe, Sammy." And he gives the tailor's appraisal of the goods. "Yeah. Imported. Custom made. I got an uncle . . . for wholesale . . . could get it."

I change into work clothes, load the cameras, pack a ditty bag, and tell Max to call me if there is anything I can do for him when he's in Dallas, and split.

Compression. That's the word that fits, as I stare at the subway posters, riding and lurching jampacked body-to-body underground on the Lexington Avenue Uptown Express. Compression's the word that fits the past few weeks and all the things that have happened and people I've met. That's the word that fits how we live today. The jet, the phone, the boob tube, the computers, the numbers of perambulating bodies create it. In a week's time you can live a year of a life, what with all the distance you can cover, people you can talk to, and coincidences that can occur. Speed reading and the Polaroid camera and the data bank and teaching machines and high-speed presses and how the hell can any one person assimilate what's going on fast enough with sufficient sense to know whether to zig or to zag.

A few hours ago I was saying good-bye to Nkume and the kids from the Mission School in Uganda, and here I am stepping out of a subway kiosk in Harlem apologizing to their cousins for my lily-white pigment.

Max's word comes back to me. "Class." And while I felt good at the time he said it, it seems empty and impotent here amid the squalor and angry stares of the ghetto. What in hell did Frost mean by "promises to keep"? Promises to whom? And why does that come to me now?

But I will shoot and walk and shoot and search and shoot until I find the thing that says it all, because I'm semi-illiterate and the camera helps me say the things I feel without hysteria, and yet with the proof that comes from something that you can pick up and hold in your hand.

It's late, and the light is fading and I'm standing on a pile of garbage in the desolation between two tenement houses trying hard to steady a long lens on a lady who is pushing wet wash out on a clothesline high above me when a voice from behind softly threatens, "You better scat, Honky, 'less you like being cut up."

There are three of them, and they mean it. They are my age, but I know that there is nothing in my experience to call upon to turn their hate into civility in the time allotted. As I turn to leave I stumble down from the rubbish. They feint as if to chase, and I scramble off leaving them laughing.

Safe on the Downtown Express I know that two years have been pissed away. And all the privies I've dug and band-aids I've opened and umbilicals I've tied and bugs I've sprayed and roofs I've thatched were so much playtime in the sandbox, so much playing tin god in the waxworks. Mesmerized I was with the adulation that comes to any nitwit twentieth-century man in an ancient and primitive culture. Two years pissed away. And now I know what Frost meant by "promises to keep." Nice going, Sam.

Chapter

Ten

I let myself in and turn on a single light so I won't ruin the view of the city through Max's big, wide window. It's a great spectacle, New York at night. I steal a brew from the icebox and decide to pass up the jar of gefilte fish, the black rye, and the frozen blintzes.

Max teased me once about eating Jewish food. "Come on. Eat a bagel. You afraid you'll get a big nose, or the end of your cock will fall off?" I laugh to myself, turn on the television, and then lock myself in the darkroom to see what happened during the day. While the stuff is hanging to dry, I try all seven channels of boob tubery only to discover that they are running the same stuff and saying the same things they were saying when I left two years ago. So I settle for some blah-blah talk show, where unknown celebrities plug their latest record or movie or book or marital contract and tell the panel-master what a nice guy he is.

I must have fallen asleep right there in the chair because the next thing I know the phone is ringing. It's Nell. Sobbing. All I can make out is that she's in a hotel in Stowe, Vermont. The meatball has split and she's alone, and she doesn't know what to do. I tell her to get some sleep and I take her number and tell her I'll call her in the morning. That's all I can do. I can't understand much, and I don't even know if what I'm saying is getting through.

After hanging up, I feel bad. I put on some coffee and try to tell myself that there is little to be done. Then I notice the key to Max's Mustang hanging right over the phone.

Hawthorne Circle is a blur of blinking lights, saw-horses, and exploded earth. I realize the mistake of taking this route because somebody somewhere has decided to "improve" the Taconic Parkway. But it's too late to cross over, so I'll ride it out.

I'm thinking about the day and getting run out of Harlem and the two years in Uganda that look from here like so much boy-scout nonsense and what it might have been like working in Vista or one of those nitty-gritty things they have in New York. Mamma has probably done more doing her part-time thing for Head Start right there in Stamford for no pay than all my flying to and fro and digging and chopping and spraying half a world away. When should you flip and when should you flop?

Pop was in the Second World War, and one of his favorite war stories was about this soldier who used to walk around all the time picking up scraps of paper. He'd pick one up and look at it and say, "This ain't it," and throw it away. After a while the Army decided he was nuts and handed him his discharge. The guy took it and said, "This is it."

Pop would howl at this joke, and we'd go along with it. But what interested me about the joke was that lots of times I felt like the soldier, only I was always looking for something else. I read backs of cereal boxes, fortune cookies, slogans on the backs of delivery trucks, the penciled scrawls over urinals, book jackets, mottoes carved on post offices and city halls, and old gravestones. I read all those big ads where companies try to tell you what great guys they are, those little redwood signs that they sell in souvenir shops that have the Lord's Prayer or some homely wisdom on them, and those signs that hang in dry-cleaning shops that say, "In God We Trust, Others Pay Cash."

I remember the old headmaster at school laughing at the Latin inscription, "Per Aspera ad Astra," because it meant, "Over the rough road to the stars." They carved the thing in solid granite and hung it over the electric elevator.

Then one time I read Bartlett from cover to cover and another book that contained a lot of Mark Twain's one-line zingers, always looking for a one-liner that could sum it all up and act as a sort of private constitution applicable in all situations and always available to help decide whether to zig or to zag.

Of course you can find some great stuff if you keep your eyes open, but the one-line constitution that seems most appropriate for a child of our times is the immortal phrase, "Look out for number one!" which was uttered to me by a state cop as he was writing me a ticket for stopping on the Thruway. A suitcase had fallen from a car driven by a lady ahead of me and I stopped and retrieved it for her. She got the suitcase and thanked me profusely as the cop was writing me a twenty-five-dollar ticket for stopping on the Thruway.

But looking out for number one is callow and crass and selfish and mean. I realize this and know that it needs tempering with other more generous and charitable sentiments, and so I keep reading and looking for a zinger that will put a little more traction in the wheels of life.

For about twenty-four hours one time, I thought I'd found the zinger in a line from Camus. So I zigged and quit college only to find out on rereading it on the way home, when the resignation was a fait accompli, that I didn't have any idea what the hell it meant. I hope, maybe, someday I'll understand.

But there is one thing I have discovered about a search like this, and that is that the zinger is not going to appear unless you know what kind of a zinger you're looking for. As I see it the zinger needs to be something that offers the promise and the way to savor all the delicious experiences that life on this planet offers, and still leave it in better shape than when found. ". . . Drink life to the lees," as Tennyson said, but I really think there is a better constitution than this Victorian salute to a Greek sailor who couldn't navigate.

So for the moment the constitution consists of a whispered aside from a Connecticut cop combined with a shred of Victorian poetry. But I know I can do better, and keep looking. Meanwhile, I have this inexplicable hunch that the zinger I'm looking for lies buried somewhere not in the words of some sage, but in the actions of the kids at the school where I went as they walk between classes and pass by a brooding bronze bust of Abraham Lincoln. Every time they walk by they reach up and rub his nose for luck, until now after all these years his nose is a brilliant gold and the rest of him is dull and brooding. I think somehow this is no insult to the memory of Abe, but rather some kind of greeting or genuflection containing a sweet homage, or acknowledgment of affection between friends or something like that. And you can't look at the statue without thinking that of all the statues of Lincoln around the world, this is the one most often visited by his ghost, and the one from which it derives the most enjoyment, and the thing that passes between Mr. Lincoln, long dead, and these smartass kids of the nuclear age is something quicker and surer than having them pore over his life filtered through the writing of musty biographers.

Again I'm driving through Burlington; only now it's

dawn and this time I'm not feeling sorry for me, but for Nellie. Progress.

There hasn't been a car in sight for over an hour now, and a light drizzle has started. I'm wondering if I can stay awake until Stowe comes over the horizon and trying to think of the ways to keep Max's Mustang pointed east. It seems like a good time to think about what I really haven't wanted to think about for two whole years; namely, what am I going to do now that I'm back, assuming I can beat the draft for three or four more years. It would probably help if I got married and had a kid. I wonder about a job, about whether I really want to shoot pictures for a living, and whether I want to be like Max or Pop twenty years from now. If I did get married, who would I marry and who would be the bride and who would be best man. Magruder, of course, but I'd like to have Max there, too.

Magruder. I'm trying to distill all I know about the little turd. What he looks like and how he talks and walks and how he laughs and how he smelled when he was a kid coming out of the millpond all covered with slime and how he would come in from the cold with snot running down his nose and how he would get Nell and me fighting each other over some stupid thing and how he locked himself in his room for a week and taught himself to play the guitar and how he picked up a tennis racquet for the first time at the club and beat the pro, and how he always calls me Sam and not Sambo, or Samuel, or Sammy. I'm trying to think of the one word that sums up Magruder the Intruder. And that one word is surprise.

Surprise is the reason I've hated his guts, and I guess it's the reason why the world moves with him. Even his arrival on Planet Earth was a goddamn surprise. After all, Mamma and Pop had already adopted Nell and me after having apparently despaired of ever having a kid of their own. And then lo and behold, surprise—Magruder. I don't exactly remember his arrival, but from family stories about it I was not delighted at the sight of him.

It isn't that the Gruder is a contrary personality. It's just that he responds to the world in ways you can never predict. I guess that's why he fakes well in soccer and hockey. He is eight steps ahead of the world, which explains why he is always wearing the trace of delight on his face. He walks into a party in progress wearing my clothes, and everybody turns. He's unaware. And goes to the ugliest girl he can find, and whispers something in her ear, and suddenly she's transformed and surrounded. I don't know how he does it.

I must have been about nineteen and Gruder about fifteen. I was home from college, a man of the world, and find that Magruder has a new thing. Birds. A bird feeder Mamma put outside the kitchen window must have kicked it off because the Gruder has become a full-fledged bird nut. Traipsing off every weekend through the swamps with a bunch of middle-aged, pruney, feathered-friend freaks wearing funny hats and carrying bird books and binoculars. I was worried about the kid since, in my opinion, he should have been hanging around the drug store reading hot-rod magazines or grabbing ass in the tall grass.

So I started spending a lot of time telling him how to make out. What it's like. What to do and what not to do. Everything I knew—which was precious little. Magruder stood there with his dumb mouth open listening to everything I said, nodding affirmatively but never inquiring. All the while I wondered if he had shriveled gonads because he seemed unmoved by my very stimulating advice. Well, months later I found out from Stanley that all the while I was giving him this very good advice he had been having at it with this thirty-five-year-old divorcee, who worked in the post office and was also secretary-treasurer of the local Audubon Society, after school every night after the four-thirty mail got sorted. And this really ticked me off! Stanley told me that Gruder never told him, that the only way Stanley found out was that he saw Gruder coming out of the apartment over the post office three nights in a row and put two and two together and then put it to Gruder. But Gruder still didn't say anything.

The thing that got me sore was that Gruder had sat there with his dumb expression letting me go on and on making an ass out of myself while he was all along learning enough to write a book. But then, I was indignant for a while because I thought he was letting down the family or something.

If it was this surprise thing that made Gruder such a

pain in the ass, it was also what made him fun to hang around with. Just before I took off for Africa, Gruder and I were with a bunch of guys on Mt. Washington. We were straggling down this day, and when we crossed the road, we came across some guys and girls who had stopped their car beside a big, flat rock. One guy had a can of orange spray paint, and he was spraying his big, greasy initials on this rock. Well, the Gruder watched this for a minute not saying a word, and finally he said to the guy, "Can I borrow that can?" So the guy gave it to Gruder and the Gruder took the can and walked away and started spraying orange initials on the guy's car. The guy came screaming up to him. "Hey, that's my car!" Gruder never even looked up. He went right on spraying, until the guy stood right next to him, boiling mad. And then Gruder looked him right in the eye and pointed, "And that's my rock!" And he put that can in the guy's hand and walked off, never looking back.

Chapter

Eleven

The car radio is picking up a Montreal station and they're playing the Schumann C Minor Symphony, which turns me on for two reasons. First, I love the arpeggio passage in the third movement, because it's so delicate, clear, and pristine. Second, it turns me on because I used to play it in a cottage at Small Point, Maine, when I was balling Gloria.

I'm tired and strapped in the bucket seat, and driving when I'm tired makes me horny. And then I get Gloria all mixed up with Nell, and that's not right and spoils the whole thing, so I turn on some fast rock and remind myself I'm just Sam Barnes, boy druid. That takes care of that. And it's raining.

The wipers are beating a monotonous rhythm. I look

up suddenly and see a phone pole bearing down on me. There is fire in my belly as I swerve on reflex, and it's past, and I stop, there in the Vermont wilderness, at dawn.

The radio is blaring, not knowing how close it came to extinction, and the wipers keep doing their dumb thing. My heart is pounding, and my knee is twitching against the door handle. So I unbuckle and get out in the rain, piss beside the road, and stretch in the rain and then crawl into the back seat and sleep.

The watch says seven fifteen when I wake up and this is funny when I think about it, because just twenty-four hours ago Pop and I were finishing breakfast in Wilton before catching the train. That all seems like it actually took place way back during the first Eisenhower Administration.

Stowe is still an hour and a half away and I'm stiff, and my face is waxy with a stubble of beard, and my mouth tastes like I had been soul-kissing a walrus.

I call Nell's number when I pull into Stowe. The Maple Leaf Inn answers and says that a Miss Barnes checked out earlier and left by taxi. So I call the taxi company.

"Yes, indeedy. We did pick up a young lady from the Maple Leaf Inn. This morning."

"Do you remember where you took her?" I ask.

"Yes, indeedy. Yes, sir. Dropped her off at the base lodge at Mt. Mansfield. Bag, baggage and skis."

"But it's raining," I protest.

"Yes, indeedy. It certainly is. This weather ain't fit for ducks!"

I thank them and hang up.

The rain feels good on my face as I get out of the car and walk toward the base lodge. I'm wondering why in hell Nell would come here in the middle of a cloud-burst. Muddy rivulets have scarred the slush on the slope, and lift chairs swing mutely from the cable, the whole thing having the appearance of a rained-out carnival.

The door of the lodge swings open as I'm about to enter, and from beneath a yellow Gloucester hat a wizened Vermont voice mutters something about this weather not being fit for ducks.

I'm inside and there is no Nell. Benches are piled on tables, and a jeaned ski bum is sweeping and raising clouds of suffocating dust. Yes. He saw somebody. He thinks she's out there, indicating the sun deck facing the slope.

And there she is on a bench close to the picture window sheltered from the rain by the overhang of the roof. She's just sitting there, cowering, defeated, wet, and forlorn in ski pants and mukluks and a little white hat with a fluffy tassel. Her skis are leaning against the building, and a little suitcase is beside her. A wet mouse.

I hold the door open and watch trying to figure out how to interrupt. Around the corner of the lodge a big diesel snowcat comes rumbling through the mud and grinds to a halt. The engine shuts down and from its cab steps a man in a felt hat, overalls, and rubber boots. He stomps the mud off his boots on the wooden deck and looks at Nellie for just a moment.

"Hope you ain't waitin' for the tow to start. Skiers all gone to New Hampshire. Snowin' in New Hampshire."

Nell shakes her head without looking up.

He walks toward me by the door muttering, "Weather ain't even fit for ducks," and he stares at me as he goes by.

I'm behind her now. She is still and unaware. When put to it I can do a pretty good mimic of the Vermont accent.

"This weather ain't even fit for ducks!"

For a second she doesn't stir. Then she turns slowly, looking up, with that wet, pitiful, anguished face, and throws her arms around my knees and buries her head between my knees and sobs. I don't feel a thing because she is a crying child, and I'm glad she is holding onto me and that my lap is finally serving some useful purpose. I press her closer with both my hands, and she sobs. But why do I have to laugh when someone is sobbing beside me? I sit beside her and look at her miserable face all wrenched in pain, and I smile at her and laugh.

She laughs back through her distorted face and says, "I'm so miserable."

"Yes, indeed," I say, and she laughs again.

We just sit there together looking at the rain and not saying anything and once in a while she gasps for breath. Then we look at one another and laugh and watch the rain.

I really want to take a shower and shave the crud off my face and give my ass a rest after all that driving, but it seems smarter to get her out of this place. So we split. Not talking, 'til we are well out of the village and on the main highway.

"Well, the way I see it, our choices are as follows. I can run you home to a nice warm bath . . . and you can . . ."

"No. Not home. Not now."

"Well, then, I can take you to a nearby saloon, and you can drown your misery in Cassis." That's wrong, too. So we drive in silence for a while longer, and then I get an idea.

"Or how about the Old Branford Inn. Remember? In Greenfield? When we were kids? . . . the big fireplace? . . . roast beef . . . with Mom and Pop . . . we'll be there by noon."

She buys this with a nod. We drive on in silence past hamlets and farms not much changed from the time when President Coolidge was inaugurated by oil lamp in the parlor of his father's house in Plymouth.

I pull off for gas in Brattleboro and tell the man to fill it up. We are sitting there with rain streaking down the windshield, and I wish there was something to say. There isn't, but I try.

"You going to order the roast beef?"

"I'm going to order the duck."

Good. She's mad now. She turns on the radio, but all she can get is blah-blah-blah and disc jockeys with speech impediments. All disc jockeys have speech im-

pediments. Their work is therapy. She shuts off the
radio in disgust. The man wants his money for the gas.
As I give it to him he tells me, "Some rain we're havin'."

So I tell him, "Yep. This weather ain't even fit for
ducks!" Nell starts laughing good now as I burn out of
there.

The rest of the way I hear all about it. A nonstop ver-
bal marathon about Justin Clarke, meatball. About how
brilliant he is and about how brilliant he knows he is
and because he knows he is so brilliant he is blind to the
fact that other people are intelligent, and how therefore
he would tell dumb lies and then get sore when he got
caught up in them, and about how he had been using
Nell for some kind of front taking her to posh affairs because she was pretty and bright, and about how much of
a gentleman he was until nobody was looking and then
he'd get lost because what he really liked was not nice
girls but easy pieces or low-down broads and how he was
like a compass needle that couldn't settle down to mag-
netic north. And about how they went to this big, messy
party at an old Vermont farmhouse owned by a kindly
fag art director, and about how Justin split as soon as
they got there and went off with this redheaded siren
leaving Nell alone to clean up the mess with kindly fag,
and about Justin coming back in the wee hours saying
he was just looking after the redhead because she wasn't
feeling too good, and about Nell running out of the
house and ending up on the steps of the hardware store,
and the local constable taking her over to the Maple
Leaf Inn, and her figuring out where I would be and

calling me. And about not knowing where Justin finally went.

Fuck him.

And now it's quiet again and I know what she is feeling as I mull over about a girl named Louisa and how I felt that day when I'd hitchhiked down to Harpswell to help her step the mast on her sloop. When I got to the front of her driveway, some guy I'd never seen before was driving out in a pickup truck. Beside him was a girl crouched down in the seat hiding her face. It couldn't be Louisa; but it was. And that's how it feels to be dumped. I was at Bowdoin, and she was at Colby and her old man owned a coal yard in Portland and had a summer place in Harpswell. It was my first love, and I knew I loved her because when I first saw her at this clambake at Falmouth Foreside and she saw me there was some magic in the way we looked at each other. And there were days and weeks that followed when I'd paint and scrape her boat and frolic in the bay and frisbee on the lawn with her kid brothers and laugh a lot. Then suddenly there was no magic. Because we'd laughed too much. And I think now that I was afraid to give her anything but laughter and help with the boat. Because you can give laughter with wild abandon, but anything more deeply felt carries responsibility. And I wasn't ready for that, but knowing that didn't make the hurt go away. How long it persists. It's a special kind of purgatory. And it feels like a part of you has to stand alone in an abandoned house forever.

Then I found Gloria, who I thought of as Goofy Glo and who imposed no strain on my wit or intellect or manners. Back when I was fifteen or so, I had thought that all of the problems in life could be fixed up if I could just get laid. So I met Gloria, and was getting laid, and discovering that all of life's problems were not disappearing. They were multiplying. And college was a freak-out with guys getting killed for God knew why in Indochina and it looked as though we would have four more years of Lyndon Johnson even though Gene McCarthy looked good in New Hampshire. To hell with it. Exit Bowdoin.

The rain is letting up as we enter Greenfield. I drive around a while looking for the Old Branford Inn, which now turns out to be a parking lot for a new A&P. Hail and farewell!

Nell doesn't say anything, so I try to explain, "It's like Tom Wolfe said," turning south and opening the glove compartment to take out a couple of Baby Ruth's. "Lunch."

But it's not working out. I've been driving too long and my ass is tired. Nell has lapsed back into a melancholy state, and we don't know where we're going, and then off to the right there's Deerfield. That's where we're going.

Chapter

Twelve

Deerfield is not Williamsburg or anything like it. It was not built by patrician dandies with illusions of nobility and restored by Rockefellers to become a museum for a gaping public. No, Deerfield is living. It's organic, alive, and has been since those earliest dirt farmers plowed the fields nearby and slept in their log cabins by night, prospering and transforming their crude cabins into houses of articulate carpentry.

Nell doesn't know why I've brought her here and doesn't care. We're both tired after hours in the car, and it's good to just get out and stretch.

I believe in ghosts. Ever since I lived in Longfellow's room in Winthrop Hall at Bowdoin. Junior year. My roommate would be off at Smith or Radcliffe on week-ends, and I'd have the place to myself. It had to be late in the night. And then there would be Henry, with his paunchy belly and bushy white beard. He wouldn't appear until I'd read a little while and would be almost asleep. I'd nod and drift on the edge of sleep and there he'd be. He wouldn't say anything, but he'd be there, and I'd know it. Then I'd sleep.

Nellie buys a couple of ten-cent pies and a carton of milk in the grocery store and we eat and drink as we walk down the street. I'd brought Max's Nikon so this gives the visit some purpose. There are six, maybe eight cars parked along what they call "the street" which is blacktop. Take away the cars and the tar road, and the scene must look pretty much as it did when there were Indians living along the river bank, and the sovereign was the English king, and Mr. Dan'l Webster used to come over and give speeches on the common. Before that, in the very early days, they had their share of Indian massacres.

Nell has never been here before, and I've only been here briefly one afternoon when we played Deerfield Academy, which is sort of right in the middle and part of the village. I didn't have a chance to look around then, because right after we beat them five to four, we had to go to tea at the headmaster's house and then take the bus back to Watertown.

But I want Nell to see the place and hope to be able to find the house that still has Indian arrowheads buried in the woodwork after two hundred and fifty years or so. Besides, there is always a chance we might be lucky and encounter a ghost or two if things stay quiet. Failing that, I should get some good shots.

It's November and the clouds are breaking, and the Great Gaffer is arranging the light to enhance the mood. New England is not just quaint countryside with unpredictable weather, but a family album all tattered and torn that tells what the nation looked like when it was young and makes you feel a certain way that must be something like the way they felt way back then. And it's a feeling that's rich and good, and if you let it work on your soul you feel something that doesn't go away. Because letting it work on your soul helps tell you who you are and from whence you came, and this is not a feeling you can get from looking at the Empire State Building or a Howard Johnson's.

So we're in no hurry and there is a zip in the air and I'm finding some nice shots because the light is dropping into the southwest and gives nice, long shadows and texture and frosty rim light.

The fresh, clear air and the brightening skies alter our mood in a way I cannot fathom. Because Nell is up. She's not standing alone in an abandoned house as she should be, but is feisty and playful. I start to conclude that she's glad to be rid of the meatball, but this doesn't figure since I know full well how hung up on him she's been for so long, and I reluctantly conclude that as long as I live I will never ever understand the barometrics of womanhood. She teases about my concentration and fidgeting with the Nikon. She cavorts when I'm setting a shot, as if she were jealous of the camera.

She runs ahead of me and stops and looks at a thing or a doorway, and finding something, she races back to interrupt and drag me off to see. Then she stops to chat with this guy raking leaves and plays "do you know?" Nell likes to put everything together. She believes that there are really only twelve people in the world and they all know each other. And I'm pleased she's doing all these things, although she is being sort of a pain in the ass and childish, but at least she isn't bawling. And my heart goes out to her and everything is beginning to work out and our spirits are being replenished by the rain stopping and this visit to Deerfield.

A song keeps running through my head and I don't know the name or whether it has any words, nor do I know where I heard it. But for now it's Nell's Deerfield song and it matches my mood, which is tender and caring and hopeful and a lot of other feelings I can't comprehend. Exquisite.

Now we are standing in front of the Williams house, all weathered and wizened. A handcrafted, bare wood cottage scaled out in perfect proportion to the human being and designed to house the simple and uncomplicated human spirit in a simple and uncomplicated time. It had been standing here since that day in 1704 when some hostile Indians came down from Lake Champlain and burned the town, killing most everybody and taking off the rest as prisoners.

Nell reads this in a guidebook and starts to move on, but I want to stay. She tries to drag me off, but I don't budge and try to tell her why.

"We're seeing it, Nell. But we're not *feeling* it."

She looks at me, puzzled.

"Go up to it," I tell her. "Put your hands on the wood. Touch it. Close your eyes and concentrate and tell me what you feel." She shrugs her shoulders and then walks shyly up the flagstone walk to the front door because it's somebody's home and what if they open the door and ask her what the hell she's doing feeling up their house.

But she's by the door now and puts her hands on the delicately carved fluting of the portal. Her eyes are squeezed closed, her face is pointed up at the sky like she can't look into the sun, and her hands are fanning all over the door.

I'm thinking she's putting me on, so I say, "Don't you see the ghosts . . . the Indian massacres . . . the shrieks . . . the smell of the fires? It's history, Nell. You're touching it. Don't think . . . feel."

She goes on like this a while longer, so I ask, "Don't you feel *any*thing?"

She stops and walks away sucking her finger. "Yeah, splinters."

I give up. We walk on, and Nell begins to look down at her feet, not stepping on any cracks in the walk, which is all humped up and broken by the heaves of the great roots of the elms and maples along the way.

"Why are we chasing ghosts?" she asks.

I don't want to go into the Longfellow thing, so I say, "Why not . . . maybe ghosts tell us where we were . . . or where we're headed. Does that sound absurd?"

She looks at me, eyes smiling, and nods affirmatively. We laugh.

I recall the night I was reading somewhere in Camus, "my revolt, my freedom and my passion." And the very next day I walked into Dean Nat Estabrook's office and told him I quit. He smacked his lips, and pulled out the bottom drawer of his desk, and stuck his foot in it. Then he looked out the window for a while and nodded a few times and stood up and shook my hand. That was all. A freshman couldn't know what all that body English meant, but by what would have been his junior year he'd know that Nat was sorry to see him go, and he'd be missed, and that Nat understood.

The sun is setting behind the trees of the lacrosse field, and our feet are weary so we sit on the steps of the church staring off into our private worlds and I'm stretching and yawning and thinking about Nat Estabrook and quitting college and I mumble, "My revolt . . . my freedom and my passion."

"My stomach . . . let's eat," Nell says. And I crack up.

I get our bags out of the car, and we check into the inn right there in the village. It's old and real, patched, worn and creaking. I pad down the hall from my room to the john and shower off the grime, shave the beard, and meet Nell for supper downstairs.

A low fire is glowing in a shallow fireplace in the

lounge and I'm having a sherry that tastes good and induces sleep. We have dinner and for laughs order duck, that's good, and Indian pudding, but there is no way that can be good.

By now we're both yawning, and on the way up to bed I find a copy of a book written by a friend of Pop's and decide this can help put me in dreamland.

The window is open, and the trees outside are squeaking from the wind. My eyelids are drooping and, though I'm only ten pages into the book, I'm about to call it quits. I think I hear a knock on the door, but it couldn't be. When I raise my eyes, there is my sister standing in the door.

She's in a long flannel nightgown. Her shoulders are hunched in front of her, and her hands are clasped over her belly. She's been crying and she looks pitiful.

"I'm cold."

"Take this," and I toss her the comforter off the bottom of my bed, which she wraps around herself squaw-style, and then she stands there looking at me.

"I'm scared," she says, finally.

"Of what?"

"I'm scared of being alone."

"I'm right here, Sis."

Now she's weeping again. "I need to be closer. I'm scared, Sammy," she weeps.

"O.K., sit down," I say, thinking she will perch on the chair. Instead she plops down on my bed and falls into my arms weeping uncontrollably.

"I want to die."

This is annoying, and I think she better snap out of it and decide to get a little tough. "That's a hell of a good idea. Just make sure you leave the body to a needy medical student." And she laughs through her sobs.

"He just left. Just walked out . . . Everybody I love . . . is always leaving. Why? What's the matter with *me?* Why do people always leave? That's why I'm scared."

I can't help remembering the way Nell used to have a fit when Pop and Mom went off on a trip and how we used to look after her, and how I'd have these feasts in the treehouse that would pep her up when she was this way as a kid. I know she should have outgrown this thing, but apparently she hasn't, so I try to explain and try to pep her up by giving her my Polliwog Speech, which I've been giving myself off and on for several years, especially when I've been depressed.

I lift her chin in my hand and take an edge of the sheet and wipe away some of the rain, and say, "It's much more than that, Nell. It's that big, red cardboard file with the black ribbon at the baby store . . . that's what scares you. Isn't it? That sheaf of forms and old letters you've never read . . . and never can *read* . . . the crazy idea that you don't deserve a place in the sun . . . that you *are* . . . because . . . who knows . . . some silly girl . . . years ago got careless. Who knows? Who cares?

"Listen, Sis. You can say that about everybody who walks the earth. Life is an accident."

She looks away for a moment and then back to me, not comprehending.

"For God's sake, kid, twenty zillion polliwogs can't be wrong . . . one made you and one made me. And when Mom and Pop took us into their house . . . through some miracle they were able to make the great Magruder! There, goddamnit, we belong . . . I'll tell you who you are . . ."

She's been lying with her head on my bare chest. I pick her head up in my hands, and I look straight into her teary eyes and tell her, "You are a *you*! A sweet, marvelous, individual, unique you. And that should be enough for anybody!"

End speech, and she's smiling gently through the last lines and I'm pleased because I've never heard the speech out loud before.

Her hand comes from under the comforter she's been wrapped in and lands on my chest, and I flinch. "Christ, what cold hands."

She says nothing, but just lies there looking into my flesh and thinking and feeling me up, and I don't know what the hell is going on in her head. I can't believe my sister is trying to turn me on, and I can't believe she isn't. But she is. I'll damn well wait and let all feelings pass because life is complicated enough as it is without this scene.

Then she drops the bomb, "Sam, I've decided . . . I want to do it."

In the split second that follows a fire explodes in my

gut and my heart is an orchestra of kettledrums and my mouth goes dry and a trickle of icy sweat runs from under my arms and my addled mind boggles and I'm looking for someplace to hide, all the while thinking how great it would be to connect, and then she looks up and says: "I want to go see Judge Haverman and all that. I want to do what you did. Find my parents and all that. Judge Haverman was in on it." Saved. As she rambles on I realize who was trying to turn on who, and I don't think she even suspects what I've been thinking and I make a very satisfactory recovery.

She tells me about how she's been thinking about this since our walk back from the hill and about how she has this idea that Judge Haverman, who was Pop's old roommate, might be willing and able to answer her questions.

"O.K. . . . I was lucky. It can be tough tracing it down. You may not be so lucky . . . You may never find them. Maybe spend weeks and months and never . . ."

"Will you help, Sam?"

"Sure," I say, and thus assured her hand moves down my chest. I'm puzzled again so I ask, "Still scared?"

"It's when I'm alone." She draws her hand back and leans on one elbow. Then her other hand is going to work on the tense muscles of my chest.

"But if I know I can touch someone . . . know they are close . . ." which tells me it's not her, it's me.

"Sam, do you think we could be lovers?" Another

bomb. I've had enough. It's got to be stopped right now.

"You're goddamn right!" I almost yell it out.

She sits up straight a little alarmed by my vehemence. "Why do you think so?"

I reach up to the ceiling with both arms and stretch every sinew I can find in my living trunk and look her right in her doe-like saucers and shout a hoarse whisper, "Because I got a hard-on!"

She looks back with this blank and bewildered expression, and she is at first embarrassed and then smiles, maybe because she's pleased. Then she sits straight up on the bed and says she's sorry and she didn't know, stealing a glance at Mount Everest as she climbs off the bed.

"Come on now, Sis. You're scared no more. Scat. Out. Tomorrow we're off on the quest."

She wants to keep the comforter, and I say sure. I'm plenty warm enough, which is a joke that pleases her, and she walks out leaving the door open, which is typical Barnes.

Chapter

Thirteen

We don't have much to say on the drive down the Thomas E. Dewey Thruway and New Jersey Turnpike which were obsolete twenty minutes before they cut the ribbons to open them. We have lunch at a formica concession on the Turnpike no man's land and pull up in front of the porticoed courthouse around three.

I shut off the engine. "Judge Haverman, we are here!" Silence. "Remember me to the distinguished jurist."

Nellie looks out the window at the forbidding temple, just staring at it for the longest time. I do not press her, knowing how hung up she is on this thing.

"Sam, I'm terrified. Come in with me."

When I reach for the doorknob, it dawns on me that she should do this part herself. You're alone when you pray and alone when you vote and forming judgments and trying to learn and discover, and it's really private and nobody's business. I decide not to let her spoil it and shake my head.

"Please, Sam, please."

I just shake my head and the more I shake the more she implores. So finally I have to get tough. "Then fight. Fight. He ain't going to tell you anything, anyway. He shouldn't." My eyes land on the statue of the blind-folded Justice holding her scales. ". . . but maybe . . . just maybe . . . even though justice is blind it may have retained its sense of touch. Or maybe Haverman can explain away the spooks. Scat!"

She cracks open the door and is about to step out but turns back looking at me with those pleading eyes.

"We made a deal, and this part is yours." I reach over, shove open the door, and just tell her, "Scram."

"Not yet, Sam."

"Now, Nellie. Now or never." I start the engine and rev the gas a little. "I mean it, Sis. Now!"

I don't know what I will do now if she doesn't get out. She does and so do I for a little stretch. She looks back at me as she's about to climb the marble steps, and halts again at the top and looks back. I wave her on and she finally disappears behind the great door.

Standing there looking at where she's just walked I think again about what happened last night, or what might have happened, or how godawful it would have been if it had happened and if Mamma and Pop ever found out. I wonder if indeed I really am and was or could in fact be in love with my sister and she with me? Was I always and had it always been so? Is this the reason why maybe I always thought of Gruder as the intruder and why I really always thought of the family as consisting of Mom, Pop, me, and Nellie, and Gruder as sort of a special house guest to whom we must be nice? I muse about how long and persistent these feelings were, and how much the thing last night was like that delicious rapture that used to come over me when I was alone in the house and would steal into Nellie's room just to let these feelings happen.

This was when I was maybe fifteen. I would sneak in and look at her pretty things thrown carelessly about the room and see where her head had lain on the pillow of her unmade bed and touch the jars and bottles on her bureau, but never dare touch the pretty, pink things that would be hanging about. Then I would sneak back out to my room with my heart pounding and my mouth dry and lock the door and be alone. And I didn't know the word then for the situation but I know it now. Absurd.

Then a woman comes out the door, down the steps and gets into the car and slams the door, looks at me and says, "Let's get the hell out of here."

I recognize the woman as Nellie Barnes.

To make sure I know who I'm talking to, I ask her, "Are you sure you want to go through with this?"

Miss Barnes hands me an empty envelope on the back of which is scribbled something. "Right now!"

"You're not scared."

"Not scared."

"Last night you were so damned scared you had me scared."

The envelope with the scribbling on it has me fascinated now, and I read the scribbling while waiting for a light to change. The scribbling is a name. An unusual name. There must be something in my expression, because she says, "What is it, Sam?"

I don't really know what it is, but looking at the name somehow takes me back to Dean Estabrook at Bowdoin, not when he was Deaning, but when he took over a history class for a week the time Kewpie Johnson got sick. Whatever is in my head is not coming into focus, but it may come or it may not.

"Nothing. The name . . . it's unusual, that's all."

We drive back up the Turnpike and haven't yet discussed where we're going, though I'd like to get these wheels back to Max. I know I've got to pay him for the mileage and the beer I stole from his icebox. I must offer him something for all I've been mooching off him, because a friend like Max is hard to come by, and Pop spent a lot of time sensitizing us against taking advantage of friendships.

Chapter

Fourteen

It is dark. I hang a right at Elizabeth so we can go over the Goethals Bridge and ride the Staten Island Ferry to Manhattan. We are first on the boat so we can be first off and have plenty of time to stretch and look at the harbor at night. As soon as I lock the brakes, we are out of the car and taking a place by the guardrail on the bow.

"Can I get you some coffee?" She says yes, and I go up to the lunch counter and get a container of coffee for her and a can of beer for me. The boat is scudding across the bay now, and I'm pleased with the motion as I balance my way down the stairs to join Nell. I turn the corner by the staircase and stop. The lady is standing alone on the prow of the ferry boat. She's facing the wind, her chin is high, and her bosom thrust out. Her hair is blowing, and so is her poplin raincoat which is open. She's not holding on, but her feet are together, and I think, though I'm not quite sure, there is a trace of a smile on her face, so I wait to make sure and it's there and I stare. I love her!

The boat is coming by Miss Liberty. I have not budged standing there sipping my beer, looking at my sister, and wondering about her and how oblivious she is to what I'm seeing and what I'm feeling. Her eyes follow Liberty as it passes on the left and her head turns to follow, and I'm caught and she smiles when she catches me, so I recover.

"Hail Athena of Samothrace! What portents do the gods reveal?"

"What was all that?"

"Winged Victory mounting the battlements of Samothrace."

As I hand her the coffee she says, "Appropriate." She sips and looks up at me. "I did it, Sam. I did it."

"It's written all over your face." I put my arm around her waist, and we stare off and watch the lights of Manhattan loom before us.

The boat ride is over now, and I don't know what to do. I would do what Nell wants to do but I don't know what Nell wants to do. Moreover, I am afraid to ask Nell what she wants to do because she might want to go home to Wilton. I'm tired and have Max's car. Besides, being at home in Wilton seems somehow wrong tonight when we are just getting started on Nell's search and all that, so I just tell her that there is an extra fold-down bed in Max's studio, I can sleep there and she can have the big bed, unless she'd rather that I leave her off at Annie Sloan's apartment so she can bunk in with her and the rest of the working-girl group. She says she wants to stay with me because she is making progress on what has now become known as The Quest. Besides, she says she couldn't stand all that girl-gossip now that she is finding out whatever the hell it is or was that she is trying to find out.

I double-park on Central Park South, put the bags in the entry with Nell, toss her the keys and go round to the garage to leave off the car. On the way back I pick up some knockwurst and sauerkraut and a couple of six packs at the deli, all the while thinking about my kid sister and what I am going to do now that I've faced certain fundamental facts about our relationship. Like suppose I find out that she feels about me like a sister feels about a brother, then what in hell am I going to do? Anyway, I better face this possibility now and save face and hurt and embarrassment and God knows what else, but no matter, one thing is certain. I love her. I think this discovery is a little like finding an envelope with a million dollars in the seat of a taxicab and not being able to tell anybody for fear that the Sheik of Kuwait will come forward and say it's his, or worse. But I own this feeling and nobody can take it away. Though it's just a feeling, it fills me with wonder and expectation about what will happen next.

The door is ajar. I push the groceries through first and

set them on the kitchen bar. Nellie must be in the john, because I hear the water running, but the door isn't closed which is typical Barnes, and the only lights on are in the kitchen and the john. The huge window facing north has no shades. The lights of uptown form what Max laughingly calls a "Murial" because he enjoys putting down a corny scene. The New York skyline is one of the world's biggest clichés, but by God you cannot deny its power and beauty.

I put away the beer and take out a pot to boil the sauerkraut and wurst. They are going to be great with beer. I find the mustard, set some plates at the bar, get out some silverware, pop open a can of beer, and flop on the big bed. Pretty soon the shower stops running. After a while Nell comes out of the john all dressed in a pretty white blouse and skirt and barefoot and asks did I get any groceries. I tell her I did and then ask is she through in the john. She is, so I kick off my shoes and peel off my shirt, which by this time could walk itself to the nearest laundry. Nell knows this too and offers to wash it in the sink and let it drip dry. I am delighted and so is the shirt.

She starts washing while I'm taking my ablutions. I can hear her outside the shower curtain and am depressed because of what I know is in my heart and at her matter-of-factness in the way she is going about a sisterly chore. When I turn off the spigot and push back the curtain and reach for a towel, she is hanging the happy shirt on a hanger and turns ever so slightly, not taking the slightest peek or in any way being giddy or discomfited, because it never was that way at home. That's just the way things are now. She is still, after all, my sister, and I have to believe that as far as she is concerned nothing is changed. As far as she is concerned.

She goes out to hang up the happy shirt, and while I have my foot on the john lid drying my legs, I call to her: "Hey, Sis, see if you can find some clean skivvies in my bag."

She rummages around and mutters about what a mess my bag is and about who taught me to pack and about how I need a maid to follow me around and pick up after me and all. Then she tosses in a fresh pair of white shorts. It's good to have some clean cloth against my skin again. Then she tosses in a clean pair of khakis, and I'm zipping them up as I step out into the room.

My beer is on the bar where she has poured it into a glass. I go over to it and take it down about halfway. I put the glass down and stand there in my bare feet and no shirt. Nell, sitting cross-legged and straight in a big ottoman that Max brought back from Marrakesh, her hands on her knees, has the damndest smile on her face I've ever seen. I smile right back. And we begin laughing.

"What's so goddamn funny?" I ask.

"We are."

I will not ask why and just say: "We are!"

"What does Max have in his bar?" she asks.

I read over the wine list, none of which is to her liking, and end up selling her a beer. As I pop off the top and begin to pour I give her my beer speech. "Drinking

beer is a very serious business. For instance, I'm not one
of those jokers who pour a beer down the side of a glass
so it won't foam up. No sir. Beer is restless. It's born in
the sunshine out in the hop fields. Then it's brewed and
stewed and bottled and cooled and turned into magic
fluid that's alive, and if it has a little foam on the top it
gives off a nice brewy bouquet that smells like the inside
of an old saloon. Here, Sis."

As I say this she has come off the ottoman to stand by
the huge window looking out across the park and the illuminated towers of uptown. As I pad across the room
carrying a couple of glasses of beer, it comes to me
about the funny name on the back of the envelope.

"That name you showed me. I remember now where
I'd heard it before!"

"What name?" she asks.

"The one you got in the courthouse. It's the same
name as a guy who used to play third base for the Yan-
kees . . . but spelled differently. I remember all this
from a history course at Bowdoin. It's a Hessian name.
Old Hessian. Goes way back to the Revolutionary War.
And most of those people settled near Trenton."

"I want to go there tonight," she says, taking me by
surprise.

"No way, Sis. We'd have to get into the County Records building, and into newspaper files, and libraries and
that may be just the beginning. Hell, this thing could
end up in Moose Jaw or Keokuk."

"Good!" she says, "to Hell with it!" and then smiles

at me with the same grin she had while sitting on the ottoman.

Now I am in complete confusion. Very carefully she raises the glass to her lips and takes a slug that would kill a horse, and lets out this burp that almost cracks the glass. So I raise my glass, kill it and cut loose a burp that sends her reeling. Then we just stand there in front of this huge window laughing at each other.

But it dies away slowly, and we look out at the view. When it's quiet, I say, "You're different, Sis."

"I know it!"

I notice her glass is empty and begin to take it for a refill. My hand is in hers and then our glasses are resting on the window ledge. I have to squeeze this hand, and I do. There is a long, breathless silence, and neither of us is moving and I don't know what to do or what she's thinking. And I hear her take a deep breath and turn her face toward mine and it's wearing that enchanting grin that I fear is mocking me, but I love it and her, and I don't care what happens. I am going to kiss it, and I do. Very gently. Tenderly. Touching only her lips. Carefully, so as not to allow any part of my body to touch hers. I let my lips linger and sweep her sweet mouth for just a moment and stand back looking at her.

"I wanted that very much . . ." I try to explain. "I suppose because it's forbidden."

"No it isn't."

We stare, searching each other's eyes. I kiss her again because she is a woman, and I adore her. There she is and she's kissing me back!

You'd think that after living with a person for twenty whole years, seeing them grow before your very eyes, knowing their every mood and tantrum and quirk and gesture and expression in every kind of unguarded moment, watching them get changed on the diaper table and seeing them pull every snotnosed, tattletale, little bitch trick, seeing their dirty underwear going into the wash, knowing exactly when they first got the curse and how they flunked math and got held back in third grade. Knowing how they looked all covered with chicken pox, and how they got carsick when reading the funnies in the back seat, and how they screamed at the sight of a tetanus needle, and what kind of hicky cream they used, finally giving up and going on a diet of wheat germ and yogurt, and suffering through a series of meatbally boyfriends, you'd think there would be no more surprises.

Well, the men who study the moon and things have this peculiar passion about what's on the dark side of the moon, and they went near out of their minds when the spacemen went around in back to take pictures. I'm unmoved when it comes to moons. See one moon and you've seen 'em all. But to the moon studiers the pictures were some kind of revelation. Yet it could never be as exciting or revealing as what is happening to Nell and me in a studio on Central Park South this night in November.

She's sitting cross-legged on the big bed with her hands on her knees, and I'm leaning against the backboard facing her and we're talking and discovering and finding out and telling and revealing with every magic word and stopping when certain tender things are said to kiss and feel and explore each other and cooling off with talk when new thoughts occur while we are playing. And finding out things we never knew before. About how she had had a rough time while at Smith after I left for Africa and she thought she was going round the bend, and her grades went sour and she thought she might be a lez which made me laugh and she went to this shrink and began to face up to feelings she had and had not understood and how Justin came along because he was going to B.U. Law School and at least he was *there*, and how that was good because he told her what to do and what to wear and took her out, off and on, and how even though she felt he was a pain in the ass he was good for her, and somehow he helped her struggle. And I tell her what I've been thinking about the night in Deerfield and ask her if she knew what the hell she was doing and she said she didn't know then, but she knows now and we start laughing in the half-light and then we talk a lot about the day and her talk with the Judge and then about whether or not she felt transformed by the thing that happened and what it revealed and how her thing was like mine and whether your outlook can suddenly change as if some kind of breakthrough you were pushing against for a long time can suddenly and surprisingly occur and we agree it probably couldn't except that in The Quest she was looking for herself and found me and vice-versa. I kiss her again and caress her for the longest time and hug her and marvel at how nearly and perfectly she fits in my arms and how her body conforms to mine, and I tell her about the time when we were teeny kids—when she was too young to remember—and I wanted to play doctor with her as the patient. Before I get the words out of my mouth, she howls and laughs. I tell the story about having her in the treehouse and ready to take her clothes off when Mamma decided to check the safety of the rope ladder. So I had this unfulfilled dream and even used to think about what it would have been like up until and even when I was in Africa.

I sit on the edge of the bed and turn on the Tensor lamp above. It shines right into her eyes, and she squints.

"Does the light bother you?"

"Yes, Doctor."

"I'll move it, then. That better? Now just lie back and relax."

She has the slightest grin, and I commence the examination. First, the forehead. No question about it, the lady has a slight fever, and I lift her wrist and feel the pulse.

"The patient is alive, quite alive." She snickers. Next I examine the tongue, all the while whistling this soft, aimless, nonsense whistle, intent on making a proper diagnosis. Satisfied that the lady has a tongue, I begin to unbutton her blouse, all the time keeping up this inane, soft whistling. She giggles aloud and says, "Stop it," and I sit upright and look at her quizzically, and then she hastens to add, "Not the examination, the whistling."

That's good. So I unbutton and, every so often, keep things lively by throwing in a whistle which sets her off, God knows why. When she's finally naked to the waist, and I see those big boobs, I cut loose with a wolf whistle that has her rolling in hysterics all over the bed. Then with great care I lay my palm on her chest taking soundings here and there, throwing in an occasional whistle which makes her laugh more. Finally the doctor realizes he is baffled and must ask, "Where, exactly, does it hurt?"

And she thinks it might be the appendix, so of course the garments must be removed to continue the examination which makes the patient very ticklish. I find that the patient's ticklishness can be calmed considerably by kissing the pretty, pink nipples of her breasts. But I'm concerned because her fever is increasing, and she is not responding to the treatment—my whistling. Wearing a most grave expression, I look up from her breasts.

"What is it, Doctor?" she asks.

"When did you first notice the onset of this condition?"

"When you peed on Mrs. Putney's head." And we roar.

I look down again holding back my laughter. "I'm sorry, my child. It's much more serious than I had thought."

"You mean—you mean—tell me the worst doctor. Will you have to operate?"

I hold my laughter in check. I stand up, look down at her, and nod yes as gravely as I can. Kick off my khakis and shorts and turn to lie beside her.

"My gracious, Doctor!" she says with the frankest stare ever turned my way, "you've changed since Mom put us in separate bedrooms."

I just lie there laughing, very naked and full of life and beside Nellie. And she is laughing, too.

I'm about to pull her close to me, but first I must tell her what I saw on the ferry when she was facing the wind—her chin was high, and her bosom thrust out, and her hair blowing, and so was her poplin raincoat, and there's a trace of a smile on her face; I stare and tell her I love her!

"Sam."

That's all she says. She looks at me for the longest time, but I know by the way she said "Sam" she loves me and always has. If I might doubt it for a second, she dispels it when she raises herself on one elbow, looks down at my face, and gives me her special grin that cannot be mocking, that can only mean that she loves me. We have forgotten the doctor game and reach for each other.

Chapter

Fifteen

It must be way past midnight. We are awake from a deep sleep and realize we've had no supper. So I boil the wurst in the sauerkraut and pour a couple of beers and set them on the bar. Nell pads out of the john wrapped in an old bathrobe that belongs to Max and sits down at the bar. I'm naked, and she watches me serve. But before I come around to sit beside her, I think it best to dress for dinner and slip into my shorts. Throughout all this I tell her about Gruder the Intruder and the thing I had about that, and about my being jealous of her way, way back when I was thirteen or so. "Here I was, two whole years older than you, and I was still a runty, hairless brat with a high-pitched voice, while you . . . you were becoming a woman!" We laugh about this and figure out the answer to some of the family brawls of this period when Pop would take her side and Mamma would be silent and Gruder would dance with glee on the sidelines. We finish our meal in silence, pausing only to touch and kiss and emit an occasional giggle.

I am cleaning up the plates telling Nell about me being such an asshole for so often being on the brink of tears, especially when I'm alone and tired, and how I'd choke up in Kumi when I'd get a letter from home, or read about some going-on back in the United States of America like Bobby Kennedy's train going through Baltimore and people singing "The Battle Hymn of the Republic" as it went by, and the slightest cloud passes over her face which one wouldn't notice in anyone except in someone you love because your antennae are otherwise not that sensitive. I do not think about it but it stays. We get back on the bed and chat about this and that. Then quite suddenly she says, "Sam I want to look at you."

"Go ahead."

"No, I want to really look at you. I want to turn on all the lights and look at you. And then I want you to look at me."

So we turn on all the lights and lie down together, and she pulls off my shorts and looks at me. I can feel her eyes as they caress and probe. It excites me and makes me laugh. She grins back and once in a while whistles softly and both of us break up. Then she asks me to lie on my stomach which sort of throws me. I have to ask her what the hell is this game.

"I want to see your asshole," she says.

I look at her incredulously, then quizzically, and she says, "And then I want you to look at mine."

"Why the hell for?"

"Because I want to and want you to. And then I'm going to give you my speech. You gave me your Polliwog Speech and now I want to give you my Asshole Speech." I relent, thinking that this is going to be the most undignified thing that has ever happened to me, but it isn't. Nor is it clinical.

When it's my turn to look at Nell in the bright light, I see her in a new way, and I have a new feeling, and when I look at her asshole the dignity thing never enters my mind and certainly not hers.

Then we turn out the lights, and she gives the Asshole Speech. It's a much better essay than the Polliwog thing—better organized and structured to reveal a completely logical premise, discussion, and conclusion. I was afraid it would be Freudian, but it's not, and I hear no trace of cribbing from the Greek or medieval philosophers. It's Nellian, eclectic, and deals with self-esteem. And I can't remember all she says but it makes me both laugh and choke up. For she says that what is felt is honest and should be faced and understood, and that we should not feel ashamed for having feelings that we suspect the world would not approve of, and that it is ennobling to face and understand feelings and demeaning to feel ashamed or guilty, and that the way I use "asshole" I do disservice to the word and to the self and most of all to the asshole.

When she finishes, I look at her. She is grinning, and my heart is pounding like an orchestra of kettledrums. My mouth goes dry, and my mind boggles as the rapture sweeps over me. I pull her close to me and tell her with all of my body what the rapture is like, and she discovers the rapture too, and it sets us free, and a new kind of sleep descends upon us that is like the suspension of life.

Chapter

Sixteen

The studio is filled with the flat soft north light of the low November morning sun. My eyes cast about taking in the functional disarray of a photographer's workshop and look over to see my sister asleep, her hair tossed carelessly on the pillow, oblivious to my gaze, and I remember the morning I came home and went to her room and how she looked then and how she looks now, and all that has passed. Gertrude Stein said about Oakland, California, "There is no there there." I finally work that out and figure that every place should have a "there,"—it is where the essence of a place resides. A church has an altar, and an altar has a center where there's a cross. A Catholic church has a candle burning and that is its "there." And a home has a "there" that can be a room like a kitchen, or a den, or a fireplace that the people of the home think of when they think of home. I laugh at the Barneses because our "there" would be in the john since most of our important conversations take place in the john.

I look at Nell and wonder where her "there" resides and know that it's there in her body probably hidden in her grin, and now I've visited her "there" and know that I love her.

I get up quietly, so as not to disturb her, and pad off to the john, closing the door softly, and shave. She's still sleeping when I come out so I dress quietly, putting on the clean, happy shirt, then make some coffee and shake some juice that Max left behind. The juice is cold and snappy going down. I pour some coffee in a mug, and filch a piece of black bread from the icebox, settle into a chair near the bed, and watch to be there when she awakens. It's hard to think of what it will be like when she wakes up because this is the first day of a new kind of life. It's filled with a whole bunch of new feelings. While they are exciting, they are a little scary because it's completely new territory. Though it seems impossible, I think she may, just may, for some reason wake up and feel badly about the thing we have done and want to erase and unsay and unlove. Because the thing we have done is not just a game played out between two kids who can go their separate ways. We are brother and sister. We have opened a door that can never be closed. And in some strange way I begin to feel it's akin to another forbidden door I've opened—my going to visit my real father—and I think of the lady who was typing by the door of the auto showroom and told me the time of day.

I continued to wonder, now about Nell waking up and things being just the way they were during the long night and about all the things we said to each other and all the things we didn't say. I realize that the most important omission concerned the manner in which our love was to be sustained and perpetuated. Whether I could indeed make it shooting free-lance and have my own pad in the city with Nell living there with me, and about people finding out, which doesn't bother me, except that Mamma and Pop are people. So if the thing is to grow and endure we must either do the sneaky-do bit or get married. And sneaky-do is not my style, and certainly not Nell's. But the whole idea of confronting my parents with the declaration of intent is discomfiting for reasons I don't understand and can't even focus on because of the persistent slamming in my face of this forbidden door. Of course I know what this is, but it apparently isn't enough just to know it. Some other thing has to happen, and I'm not going to think about it now because I don't have to. When put to the test, I can procrastinate better than most anybody.

But if contemplating making a declaration of intent to my parents fills my heart with terror, doing the same to Nell fills it with joy. She stirs and gives a slight yawn, her eyes opening slowly and casting about to see the empty place beside her. A shadow passes over her face. Then she looks up and sees me sitting in the chair gazing at her, and the burst of smile when her eyes fall on me. I don't let a second pass.

"We could marry," I say.

"We shall."

And that is all that is said about that. I give her coffee in bed, a slug of juice, and a crust of black bread, and we talk not at all. She stretches and I clear the dishes and hear her go into the john. She starts to sing as she turns on the shower.

"I want you to scrub my back."

A college kid once set the all-time shower-taking record and I think it was five days or so. Solo. But Nell and I set the dual record, though I don't bother to clock the exact time, because there is so much to say about the day and The Quest and where to go and where we've been. The Quest can wait, which surprises me. And for now it is home, and ours is the secret.

Then when we have lived with the thing that we know for a while and get our bearings there will be the declaration, but I must not tell her about my terror of this.

She asks me why I laughed last night when she was telling me about her coming unstuck at college and thinking she was a lez. I tell her I laughed because there was a time way back when I was sure I was queer because I didn't like football and parties and dancing and all those machismo, four-square, all-American things. Instead I liked to read poems and play square music. All of this was bad enough, but the clincher was that I was not above looking at other guys in the shower at school to see how they were hung. This gives us a good laugh as we dry each other and dress and pack and lock up and catch the Wilton Express.

Chapter

Seventeen

There is an old lady in the front seat of the cab we take from the station who has to be let off at a new street with new houses that have been built since I've been away. Then we back-track and turn up Olmstead Hill Road and come to a stop in the driveway beside the house. While Nell gets out, I pay the driver and go round to the trunk to get the bags and watch her go in the back door. I was fidgety in the cab coming up, but not Nell. So instead of following her in, I decide to go round front and race for the stairs, in the hope of deferring forever a meeting with my parents. I am three steps up the stairs when I hear Pop behind me.

"How did it go?"

"Huh?"

"How did it go? . . . Is she O.K.?"

"Who?" I ask, which wins all-time first prize for dumbshit answers to perfectly legitimate questions.

"Nell!" I can't really blame him for sounding irritated. "What happened to what's his name?" he asks.

I shrug the last question and answer the first. "Yeah, she's O.K." And turn and get out in a hurry. I drop Nell's bag in her room and return to my own and lay out the bag to unpack, and am about to sigh a faint sigh when he's standing there.

"How'd you make out in the city?"

"What . . . ?" If he sees how startled I am by the question he doesn't show it . . . But I must believe he knows I am startled.

"How'd you make out . . . find a job?"

I shake my head, not looking at him.

He respects my privacy, and I am grateful to him for that.

"Well, there's no hurry. Take plenty of time, and don't take the first thing. Decide what you want and go after it."

In the long pause that follows he watches me first putting away my laundry in a sack and then hanging clothes. When I come back from the closet, he's looking out the window.

"I'm taking your mother out to a convention at the Broadmoor next week, so in the meantime if there's anybody you want me to get you in to see . . ."

He lets this trail off and turns from the window. "So you think Nell's taking this pretty well?"

I resent this hovering over-concern with my kid sister. She is now a grown woman and in love with a man who wants to marry her, and she him.

"She's got to get away from here."

"Not a bad idea . . . we can take her along to the convention . . . do her good."

"No! . . . you can't do that. I mean, she ought to move out." I'm getting my please-Daddy-I'd-rather-do-it-myself voice again. "And I don't want my old man worried about lining me up with anybody for a job." Machiavelli said don't just punish your enemies. Crush them.

"Well, well . . ."

"I'm sorry, Pop. There's just a lot of things I gotta get sorted out."

I realize that I'm trying to hurt him so he will hurt and punish me. But he somehow understands the ploy and destroys my plot with one gentle gesture. Putting his big hand on the back of my neck and shaking it gently like he always did.

"Take your time . . . Who was it said, 'Growth is gradual?' "

I know it was Gibran but just answer, "Well, I'm just trying to increase its velocity."

He smiles and, before leaving, asks me to get the grocery list from Mamma because she has some errands she wants me to run in the village before supper.

So I have just pushed my grocery cart down the pet food aisle and am heading for the checkout counter, when I hear my name called out and turn to stare into a face that I don't know, but do. Somewhere. Way back, but different now. A girl in pigtails and bare feet, bearing faint resemblance to the Meg Benbow I knew years ago. No longer the fidgety, little ugly gamin with quicksilver eyes that scampers away for fear of being spoken to. Now she's standing before me with both bare feet planted firmly on the floor, telling me she has just heard from Magruder. And I realize that she must be "Whatsername," a designation Magruder has been dropping into his letters from time to time which I assumed referred to some mythical chick who would be sort of a placebo to hanker for while he was doing time in the boonies. So there is a real "Whatsername." And she is obviously the one to be included in the April trip to the Rockies.

Her mother is a widow who writes poetry and some stories for magazines, and when I was a kid I had a sort of sneaky for her mother. I used to go over to her place to do the lawn, and clean up the yard, clear the gutters, and help out around the place for seventy-five cents an hour, and all the while her mother would be on the sun porch typing. And then around noon she would invite me into the house for a lettuce and tomato sandwich and a glass of iced tea, and we would talk. I guess the reason I liked talking to Mrs. Benbow is that she talked to me then (I was only about sixteen or so) like I was a grown man. She'd talk about politics or music or books and ask my opinion about this and that and pay me compliments by suggesting I read stuff that most people would think was way over my head; I always was surprised that around her I felt like sixteen going on forty-seven. There was this one time when, in a very matter-of-fact, offhand way she started talking about the pill and wondered aloud whether for young people oral sex wasn't better than meddling with body chemistry. I began to unravel. And all the while little Meg would be in the background darting in and out and hearing everything and, I assume, absorbing everything that was said and unsaid. But in the process of unraveling I didn't know whether to zig or to zag, because if I zigged I might have solidified a beautiful friendship and if I zagged I might have destroyed it. So I compromised and asked for another glass of iced tea and then accidentally spilled it all over my pants and went out and hung a bird house in her apple tree.

While we're checking out, I invite Meg to join me at the drug store across the street for a cup of coffee. On the way over I'm appalled at the toughness of her bare pads on the cold pavement; all the while she's babbling on about the Gruder, about my stint in Africa, about Nell and Mamma and Pop.

Over coffee it comes out about the proposed trip to Aspen, and I'm beginning to learn something about what has been going on between them, which cannot be a hell of a lot because geography has made the relationship totally literary. It comes out that, indeed, this is the case because the thing began to flower just before he left for overseas and, somehow, grew because she was pretty deep into the Peace thing and he was on his way to the War thing. Now she is excited because he is coming home soon. I ask all about her mother and how she is getting on with her writing, and Meg mentions a brief, unhappy marriage her mother tried a few years back. As I leave her there in front of the drug store, she asks me to stop by soon. I drive off thinking I have to impart some very good advice to my nineteen-year-old brother before he spins a web of complications from which he may well find it difficult to extricate himself. At the same time I'm surprised again at the Gruder's remarkable perception in discovering a mother lode of sweetness and sensibility behind a face that is not very pretty. I can't help but remark on the wit that flashes, and the flourishing self-mocking intellect so rare in a high-school senior. And decide that someday soon Nell and I will have to call on the Benbows to renew a thing that is hard to find.

The Dutch King had granted title to the lake and most of the country to a patroon family when Peter Stuyvesant was still Governor of New Amsterdam. It remained unspoiled and primeval through all the centuries of expansion and exploitation. And just when some Babbitt from Scarsdale was ready to move in with bulldozer and chain saw and introduce it to "progress," it was snapped up by a friend of Pop's who made a lot of money in broadcasting. Everybody around there called him The Squire and wondered what he was going to do with this haven of wilderness. They wondered even more when he gave it to his friends on condition that it would remain then and forever as it was. No motorboats or cottages or pop stands, no chopping trees, no improvements.

But there's nothing in the deed about ghosts. And you know whose ghost is living there now that Walden Pond is all messed up? Guess.

I like to troll and cast from a canoe around sunset. Today I am paddling and Nell is casting, and my own line is trolling and bobbing in the wake. I hope we don't catch anything because I don't want to be interrupted.

"What did Pop say?" asks Nell.

"He said, 'Growth is gradual.' "

"What did you say?"

"I said I'd like to accelerate its velocity."

Then I spring the idea I'd had in the back of my mind all along. "We could elope."

"We couldn't. Mom and Pop would die."

"They've known for years we've had some kind of a thing."

"They have?"

"Hell, why do you think they kept shoving me off to summer camps and schools . . . and remember how fast Pop got behind the Peace Corps idea."

"All the more reason why they should have their say."

"But we both agree there's nothing wrong . . ."

"And there isn't. But we don't know what they think and they may think there is—no, Sam, we have to face up."

"Mr. Barnes . . . No, . . . Father, I want to marry your daughter—better still, Hey, Pop, can I marry my sister? Oh Nell, we didn't get their permission to consummate it, why do we need their permission to legalize it?"

Then with the precision and finality of Nell, "Because other people's feelings are involved."

The light is fading rapidly, and it's getting colder. Nell reels in the plug and changes to a spinner as I paddle back to the dock. But first I paddle by a strip of sandy beach behind some reeds on the north end to see if the ghost of Henry Thoreau is still camping there. He sure enough is, and I smile. Nell wonders why, and then she smiles because now she's aware he's there, too. She hops to the dock and steadies the canoe by grabbing my paddle, I hop ashore and together we pull up the wooden canoe which, unlike most, was not made in an airplane factory but in a shed in Old Town, Maine. There is silence as we take a last look at the still lake which has a life and surely a mind of its own. It has to be wise, it's so old.

It's an hour drive back to Wilton down Route 33. I tell Nell that I know she is right about eloping and that there will be a facing up and the declaration. But I also explain that the declaration is not enough unless it's backed up by some intelligent thought given to how the bride is to be maintained in the manner to which she is accustomed. That means getting into New York and getting a job that earns enough bread for two. This is sad because it means riding the rails every day and pounding the streets trying to sell Huckleberry Camera. The uncertainty of making a quick sale depresses me, but Nell fires back saying I should not come home at night, but stay at Max's to save time and money, and talk to everybody I know day and night and plead and beg and cajole and fight and that way the time will pass quicker and I'll get a job faster. I laugh because she just gave her Job Speech. But she is right.

The folks are out to dinner at Ferguson's when we get back. Nell finds some good cheddar rat-cheese in the ice-box and whips up a rabbit for supper. If you look it up in a cookbook, you can't find a recipe for Welsh Rabbit because in the cook books they call it "rarebit," which is wrong. Nell pours the whole mess over broken-up soda crackers in two big platters, and we make a toast with two beers and eat. When we're cleaning up, the folks come back. I stun the old man by asking him to go over my list of the people I want to see in the next week about finding a job. He wants to know what happened, and I tell him about Nell's Job Speech, but not all about it. I think maybe I've tipped my hand too far. For just a second his eyebrow raises. A thought must have crossed his mind that something unprecedented was happening. But it's his style to believe what is said or at least to pretend to believe it and make his own judgments in silence. We sit at the kitchen table and go over my lists. He surprises me with the number of people he knows and what he knows about them, about whether they are genuines or fakes, and about what kind of approaches they might respond to. Then he gathers up the Sunday *Times* and pads off to bed.

I try selling Nell on a date at the movies thinking we could be off and away for the evening. No sale. The house is quiet with Mamma and Pop reading in bed. We put on a new recording of Mahler's Fifth that Nell bought and we settle down for a quiet evening at home, Nell sitting in the easy chair in the living room that we always thought of as Pop's, and me sprawled out on the floor facing her and loving her and wanting her.

The finale reaches its crescendo, and the machine turns itself off. I get up to put away the record, turn and face Nellie and hold out my arms. She comes to me and we kiss. Then she breaks away grinning and saying good night and shooting out the door which I think is a little too abrupt, but suddenly she pops her head back in and says that that's the last one we'll have 'til I'm gainfully employed. She grins again and leaves. Alone.

Chapter

Eighteen

The city is wide awake when I get off the train and begin to make calls for appointments from a phone booth in Grand Central. Most of the people are kind; the last even asks me to come right up, which I do. The stores along Fifth Avenue are showing their Christmas wares, and I think of Mamma saying how shocking and greedy it is because Thanksgiving isn't even here yet and already they want you to think about Christmas. Then it dawns on me that Thursday is Thanksgiving. It will be a short week, and most everybody will be too preoccupied with their own plans to think about hiring a cub photographer. But I tuck my portfolio under my arm and press on. The day is spent in reception rooms, buses, phone booths, and offices sitting on the edge of a chair while some guy picks up a picture and then another and another, musing and sniffing, sometimes saying nice things and sometimes not saying anything and sometimes giving "advice" which is another way of telling you their life story. When I turn the key in Max's studio this night, I feel satisfied that I've been able to get two no comments, three B-plusses for composition, an A-minus for insight, and four life stories. The A-minus pleases me the most, because the guy liked my favorite shot that nobody else had even noticed. A-minus thanked me and told me there was nothing available now, but that he'd keep me in mind in case anything turned up. I fish out a beer and pour it into the glass that Nell used "that night" and turn it around in my hand wondering how I can get to talk to her without causing too much alarm. Then the bulb in my brain lights up.

Mamma comes on the phone. I tell her things are O.K. and that I still have another guy to see who was at the wire service when I was there, that yes I can get a good meal, that yes I won't stay out too late, and yes I have enough money. I ask if Pop is there because I want to tell him what's going on. I give him a brief report, which needs a little embroidery to make it sound like it's worth the phone call, and mention how I ran into a friend of Nell's on Fifth Avenue and is she there because I'd like to tell her about it.

"I did not meet Anne Sloan on Fifth Avenue today."

"Oh?"

"But I told Pop that I did."

"Oh."

"So I could talk to you without causing too much alarm back there."

"Oh, what did she say?"

"Who?"

"Anne Sloan."

"She didn't say anything; I didn't see her."

"And what did you say?"

"I love you."

"Oh."

"I miss you."

"Oh."

"Can't you find anything more to say than that?"

"No."

"You're a cruel bitch, Nellie Barnes. A cruel bitch. Isn't that true?"

"Yes, indeedy."

"And you still do love me, don't you?"

"Yes, indeedy."

"And miss me?"

"Yes, indeedy."

"Will you stop giving me that 'Yes, indeedy?'"

"Yes, indeedy."

"Good night, my sweet."

"Yes, indeedy." Click.

The guy from the wire service I am supposed to meet for a drink after dinner is there when I arrive at CB's. Loaded. I suffer through his monologue about how badly he's treated, getting aced out of assignments by some punk kids, about how his wife doesn't understand him, about how he's got this idea for selling soap like a candy-gram, and about how when he gets rich and famous he's going to tell 'em all where to shove it. That makes it five life stories for the day. Good night.

The lights of the city seem to shiver in the November cold, but it's good to be out of the saloon and into the air. On the way back to the studio I count six bookstores—four dirty and two clean—and seven movies that break down in about the same proportion. Walking alone among these bustling strangers I wonder if it's pleasure they're seeking and, if this is so, why are they seeking it in this desolation. My mind goes back to the bookstores and movie houses and what's dirty and clean and, by God, I don't know. The thing that Nell and I have is clean. How could it be otherwise? Yet I'm not telling the world, least of all our folks. To tell them would hurt them and cause needless worry and God knows what else. "Other people's feelings are involved," said Nell. There are some things a person doesn't tell anybody, sometimes not even oneself, I suppose. I wonder what things I wouldn't even tell Nell.

I pass by people with beards and burns and minis and maxis and mods and leather and sandals and tresses and Afros and an occasional serge worn with white socks and black shoes, and realize I am a square. I have no badge or emblem or tattoo or armband or shades or headband or mustache or buckle. So nobody can tell at a glance that I think we should stop the war, and legalize pot and clean up the slums and free the blacks and end the draft and cool the military and save the railroads and dump the SST and reform the courts and streamline the post office and scrape the barnacles off the Congress and register guns and stop draining the swamps and muffle motorcycles. I'm obviously square. My badge is no badge. I had a beard in Africa for a while, but it itched so I shaved it off.

Tuesday is like Monday except that I encounter no A-minuses and I run out of appointments by four o'clock. The Job Speech called for using every minute of the day and night in the pursuit of the objective, so I come back to Max's studio to make calls and set up dates for the next day. An hour of phoning nets me one three-thirty meeting on the day before Thanksgiving. Frantic now, because I'd wanted to make a triumphant return with a job and make the declaration at the Barnes's Thanksgiving Day feast. I fill Nell's glass and sit in the dim light thinking and feeling how I'm letting her down, wondering whether I'll ever be able to work in the system and make it come out all right for me and for Nell and whether the system can really be made to work for everybody and whether the system really has self-correcting devices built into it or whether it has to be taken apart and reassembled, mindful of the human needs that the system now ignores. I pace the floor and drink my beer and wonder about all these things and find myself studying Max's bookshelf, which I'd never noticed before. He has the usual photo-trade stuff—a few bound, esoteric camera books, a copy of *Standard Advertising Register* so he can tell who's who at the agencies today, and a big fat volume called *Index to Ad-*

vertisers and Corporations. I don't even think about the
ethics of the thing or whether the hippie guy on the railroad train really meant it and said it only to be kind. Or
said it just on the spur of the moment and that he probably couldn't do it even if he wanted to, but I need
help. There it is. Great Eastern Industries and the
Chairman of the Board whose name is not really that
difficult to pronounce, if you break it down into sixteen
Armenian syllables. The son's name is Vic and, yes, he's
in the Manhattan directory.

"Who?"

"Sam Barnes of the late, lamented New Haven Railroad."

"Yeah, hello Sam. How you doin', man?"

"I'm in trouble and need help."

"What's the matter? You need bail?"

"Worse than that. I want to go to work for your old
man!"

He says that remark is funny; he'd like to help, but he
can't make any promises. But his old man owes him one
and he'll call him right now and if he is home he'll speak
to him and can he call me right back? And he does. Exactly three and a half beers later. "Be there at three
thirty tomorrow." Yes, indeedy.

I want to call Nell right away, but if I do and it
doesn't work out, which it probably won't, it will be bad
and depressing. Anyway I've got to have some ploy to
get her to the phone so the alarm won't go off and I've
used that met-an-old-friend bit already. But I must hear
her voice and make sure everything's the same. I'm pac-

ing the floor and looking out at the night sky and the skaters in Wollman Rink. That's the new ploy. It's weak, but it will work. Buzz, dial, ring, ring, ring, click.

"Hello."

"Hi, Pop."

"What's up?"

"I got two meetings at three thirty tomorrow."

"Oh?"

"We'll see . . . is Nell around? I got an errand maybe she can run for me tomorrow before the holiday. I want her . . ."

"Right here . . ." his voice trails off. I can see Nell coming to the phone and I wonder what she's thinking, and how she looks and what she has on and if maybe she's thought it all over and decided . . .

"Sam?"

"I love you."

"How much?"

"I miss you."

"How much?"

"The ploy of the day is called getting Nell to take my skates to be sharpened."

"Yes, indeedy."

"Will you cut out that 'Yes, indeedy'?"

"Yes, indeedy." Click.

Chapter

Nineteen

It's eight ten now, and there is just time to grab a hot dog at Chock Full O'Nuts on the corner of Fifty-seventh Street and then beat it over to Carnegie Hall and maybe grab a single or a standing room ticket before the band starts playing. Cleveland is in town and they are doing the Prokofiev C Major and some Schubert stuff and what Nell calls Mozart's Jumping Jupiter, only she really calls it the "Yumping Yupiter," which derives from a Swedish day, which I'm thinking about as I'm eating my hot dog.

We used to have days, Nell and I and the Gruder. There would be Swedish days and French days and Chinese days and Italian days and Spanish days and Swahili days when we would talk to each other in dialect all day long at whatever we were doing and even at meals. The Gruder was the best mimic and kept us all in stitches. One day, when it was Scottish day we were sitting around the table having lunch and we were all of us trying to keep up with the Gruder's brogue and all the talk was of whiskey and heather and fair lasses and the mist in the Highlands and pass this in brogue, and Magruder starts telling this bawdy story about a man named Sandy McFee who got drunk "and lay doon in the heather to sleep and along cooms two Hi'lan lassies," and on and on 'til he comes to the punchline and says it, and Pop nearly explodes and stamps his feet and howls and laughs and stamps some more and turns all red in the face and tears come to his eyes and he starts to choke and gets up from the table and goes out on the lawn holding his side because it hurts so much.

The Gruder could make Pop laugh anytime. Pop liked it best when the Gruder would get out his guitar and sing limericks and nod to Nell. Then the two of them would sing sad folk songs and ditties and show tunes and Pop would listen and wonder and applaud.

This band plays the Prokofiev like Steuben makes crystal. It sparkles and flashes and dances with light. And, of course, they make the Yupiter yump.

My mouth is dry as I walk away from the hall and decide to stop off at a bar on West Fifty-eighth Street in a neighborhood that Max calls Vaseline Alley, because this is where kept women are supposed to be kept.

The muzak is playing, and there are a few men and

women standing around the bar drinking whiskey and trying to promote things. Others are sitting at tables and getting bombed and wasting time. It's not pleasant compared to where I've come from and what's in my mind, so I finish my beer and get out.

I stand by the studio window looking out at the Murial thinking about all the good things that are happening and might happen, especially if old Jawbreakian comes through. I'm tired and recall a flute passage from the Schubert thing that Cleveland played tonight and my eyes well up and I have to remember the Asshole Speech so I won't feel ashamed of the way I feel. And I realize how grateful I should be for the good things that are coming my way now that I'm back home. Then I think about something I haven't done, really done, since I was a little kid. I don't think I better do it because I haven't done it in so long it is probably fake. But I decide that even though it may be fake I'm going to do it anyway, because the worst that could happen is that Max would walk in and catch me. So I kneel down by the big bed and say thanks.

Chapter

Twenty

It's a rainy morning. There's nothing to do but call to cancel the other three-thirty appointment and then wait 'til three-thirty to go over to Jawbreakian's. So I decide to get some air, and look at the store windows, and then come back to make the call. I should really stay on the phone all day so as not to act contrary to the principles set forth in the Job Speech.

My hand is on the doorknob ready to leave when the phone rings and I rush to grab it. A-minus thinks he has something that might be interesting and asks if I could be at a studio on the West Side at three thirty? No, I can't. What do I mean I can't; this is a job, man, and no it can't be any other time, but when am I free and he'll

check and call me right back. And he does and will two
thirty do? Set.

At two thirty I'm sitting in a paneled reception room
near a sliding glass window where the telephone-switchboard-reception girl sits chewing gum and reading *Photoplay*. At three ten I'm still sitting in a paneled reception room next to a sliding glass window where the
telephone-switchboard-reception girl sits chewing gum
and reading *Photoplay*. "I'm sorry," I say. "Good-bye."

It's raining hard, and not a taxi in sight, not even a
bus. Jawbreakian is on the other side of town, and you
can't hitchhike in the City of New York because it isn't
done, so I run.

At three twenty-seven I stand soaking wet just inside
the World Headquarters of Great Eastern looking for
the illuminated directory which tells you where everybody is. But there is no illuminated directory, only a
small bank of elevators that go I know not where and a
few men standing around in blue business suits, white
shirts, and identical Black Watch ties. A man in a blue
business suit comes up to me and peers into my eyeball
and asks, "May I help you, sir?"

"I'm looking for the directory."

"Whom did you wish to see?"

I almost say Jawbreakian, but manage to get it right.
He points to an elevator that is manned by a man in a
blue business suit, a white shirt, and a Black Watch tie.
The doors slam closed and pop open again, and the
other man says, "Did you have an appointment,
sir?"

"Three thirty."

He asks my name, and the doors pop closed. The doors pop open, and I'm somewhere else. There's a lady with gray hair standing in front of me, and she says, "Mr. Barnes?"

"Yes."

"Come this way."

I follow her down this long passage with a thick, black rug and there is a paneled wall of solid mahogany on one side and pinpoints of light from above to show the way. All you hear is the whir of the air conditioning and the quiet sound of distant typing which for an instant reminds me of a scene in an auto showroom in Vermont.

She tells me to please sit in a big semicircular leather couch in front of a big, low circular, black glass-topped table and read *Forbes* and *Fortune* and *Business Week* and *Business Management* and *Natural History*. What the hell is that doing here?

But first I take off my coat and hang it up. I'm soaked clear through and out of breath, and I'm calling myself a jerk for coming so close and then blowing the whole thing.

A man comes out and says he's Mr. Jawbreakian's secretary, and asks if I mind waiting just a moment longer because Mr. Jawbreakian is on the phone to Tokyo and will be free shortly. He goes away.

I take out a handkerchief, wipe the water off my face and the mud off my shoes, and notice my flesh showing through the wet cloth of my shirt and a voice comes out of the shadow. He is perfectly framed. There is just enough light coming from a standing lamp to show the detail of the face, and the pinpoint beam above his head puts a sharp edge of rimlight on his steel-wool hair.

"Mr. Barnes?"

"Yes."

He tells me his name and gives me his hand. I'm embarrassed already because his is warm and dry and clean, and mine is wet and clammy and dirty.

I tower above him as he leads me into his office, and he is standing with his back to me as I get settled in a chair by his desk. He starts to fill his pipe and says, "Well, well, well, well, well, so you're a friend of Victor's."

He turns back toward me smiling, and his soft black eyes take in everything in front of him. "Tell me how you met."

He speaks so softly and his accent is so thick that I barely understand. He sits in his chair, almost lost in its size, and tucks one leg up under him, all the time sucking his pipe and nodding. I hasten to explain that I really don't know Victor. I tell him about the train and about the kids. Then I apologize for taking up his time and intruding like this, but I explain that I have this girl, and we want to get married, and I want to make the declaration and on like that for a while 'til I find a way to stop because the speech is getting to sound too hysterical. There is a pause and I notice some shots of Vic on the table beside him and now know what Vic looks like sans beard. There are also some shots of him and his wife after their transformation. The old man continues to suck his pipe and then starts to talk. He talks about Vic, and sucks, and says a few more words, and thinks and sucks some more, and talks and thinks some more and talks. I'm beginning to understand more of what he says; and it's mostly about Vic dropping out and how it upset his mother. Then he stops, looks at me, and says, "I think it's marvelous."

I can't believe it. Before I have time to think about it he says: "Tell me about Sam Barnes."

I do, because by now I've heard enough life stories to know how to tell them.

I keep thinking it's time to leave, but he gives me no sign. The phone never rings, and he wants to know what I think about the new government of Kenya and what's happening in Ghana. He asks me what I think about Vic and the way that he lives. I explain about my badge and somehow though I think it's dumb to let on, he gets me to tell him what I feel about slums and blacks, the Congress and swamps and all the rest. All the while he sits on his leg and nods and sucks and then there is no more talk, and I've blown it and it's time to go but I don't know how.

"How much do you need to get married?"

He laughs when I tell him. He fills his pipe and tells me that his company's problem is that it's full of old men, that they probably don't need a photographer, and that he doesn't know where I'd fit in. I'm glad it's over because it's getting late and I want to get home to see Nell even though I can't touch her. Then he says, "A year."

It figures that he wants me to come back in a year, and I stand because this must mean it's time to exit. Then he stands and says it again, "A year. Starting Monday. I don't know exactly what you will do, but you will find that yourself if we have it. I think you have what we want, but it will take a year for us to find out what it is. Maybe ten."

And as I pass out of his door he calls one more time, "Oh, Mr. Barnes."

I look around and see his secretary helping him into his overcoat. His hat is already perched on top of his head with its brim upturned. "Welcome to the establishment!" I smile back and leave, but I mustn't skip or jump 'til I'm outside, for that would be unseemly for a new employee of Great Eastern Industries and all its divisions and subsidiaries, Amen.

Mamma answers the phone and I only have time to say that I got one and am running to catch the 6:02 train and to ask if Nell can meet me in Darien and hang up.

By the time I've taken eight blocks I realize it's raining and that I haven't even buttoned my raincoat and I laugh and look up into the sky and let the rain wash my face and fall into my mouth and I taste it and it's clean and cool and my mind rushes forward, thinking about how everything is falling into place and thinking how all this is happening because I said thanks. So I laugh again and look up at the rain and say thanks again. And think for a moment and say thanks again for giving the rain because it feels good on my face and tastes good in my mouth and is washing the world clean.

I stop by the deli in Grand Central, buy a couple of cans of beer, pick up a copy of the *Post*, pad off to Track seventeen and down the ramp and onto the steaming train, through two, three, four, smoldering stuffy, jampacked cars, stepping by standees, guys sitting on briefcases, guys leaning against doors crowding onto the platforms and by one knowing guy who has his own campstool from Abercrombie & Fitch. Finally I settle for a seat on the sink in the ladies' room and laugh because this is typical Barnes. Two other guys are standing in the men's room.

It's bad form to stand in a train toilet all the way with the door closed. Also it smells. So I shove a folded paper towel under the door, perch on the sink with my feet on the john, pop the top off my beer, salute the two guys in the men's room across the aisle, and silently toast my bride.

The train is underway and by the time we are out of the tunnel, my first beer is gone, and my head and my innards are reeling with some kind of good feeling which is not like being high, but comes from elation. The feeling is splendid and braces the mind. I smile as the conductor-priest punches my ticket and offers a benediction. Then I go back to those sweet thoughts about who is waiting for me when I get off the train and about what I will say and what Nell will say and how pleased

the old folks will be and about how they will be overjoyed to discover that their son not only got a job but
also discovered his sister and the jokes that will follow
and how Pop will crack a corny joke like, "I'm not losing a daughter, I'm losing a son!" and how the ladies
can giggle and gab and plan a wedding for when the
Gruder gets back, which should be soon after Christmas, because we've known each other for twenty-odd
years and who needs a long engagement. And for just
one split second I think about Louisa and what she will
think. To hell with all that, I've got Nell.

Greenwich is passing by. As I finish the other beer,
the thought occurs to me that perhaps the folks are not
going to be overjoyed. And I supposen this and supposen that and wonder if I'm not racing my engine too
much and realize I'm not even in gear. I again think
about eloping and think about the Asshole Speech and
the Job Speech and decide not to think about anything
else until I see Nell.

I must write Vic to tell him about how things worked
out and tell him how grateful I am to him for sticking
his neck out for a stranger, how he can be sure I won't
let him down, and ask him about getting together with
him and his wife when Nell and I get settled in a pad in
the city.

"Station stop, Darien!"

She's there! Grinning. Kissing. Holding! Hugging!
Now walking fast to the Green Debris and getting in
and kissing again. And talking and laughing all the way
home.

"Is it what you want?" Pop says when the smiles have faded and the laughter has died.

I'm stunned by the question and hasten to reassure. He leaves for a moment to pour a little more whiskey into his glass and add some water.

"Well, you're still young. I just hope you're not taking it to please me. You're not selling out, are you, Sam?"

"Renting, perhaps, but not selling."

I tell the story of the run through the rain to get to Jawbreakian's on time. I describe the automated men in blue suits, the automated elevator doors, the automated secretaries, and the high drama of the chairman's chamber, with him sitting on his foot and puffing his dirty old pipe. While Mamma fixes ham omelets, Pop tells about a new letter from Gruder and how he has finagled a deal to get home earlier—maybe in time for Christmas. With that Pop opens a bottle of champagne as Mamma serves supper. Everybody toasts the job and the Gruder and the omelets, and we laugh because Mamma slipped a burp, which is not her style.

Nell and I do the dishes. When Mamma and Pop leave the kitchen, I catch hell for not coming out with the declaration during dinner. I explain that it's a long weekend and that there's plenty of time. They are tired and tomorrow's Thanksgiving. There will be cocktails before dinner and wine with the meal and that's really a better time. I tell her I'm not chicken, the first lie I've told to my love.

Chapter

Twenty-one

When I come down to breakfast the turkey is trussed and sitting in a pan all ready to pop into the oven. Mrs. Norton, who has come in to help, is peeling onions and crying and laughing with a piece of bread in her mouth. Nell is cutting green beans, and Mamma is kneading the dough for fresh rolls. They let me have coffee and a piece of toast then and run me off to get a fire ready in the fireplace. Pop comes in and kibitzes as I'm setting the logs and tells me clean out the stable, then joins me in the shoveling and scraping and carrying and not talking but just being near, which he likes and I like too. After we throw fresh hay on the floor, I saddle up Pot Luck and take off down the draw and through the pines behind the reservoir, and across the meadows heading toward the high ridge up behind Millstone Road. I rest on top and look about. The sky is clear and I can see the Sound and across the valley to farms and houses and woods and fields broken by stone walls that have been there since the first farmers came and settled here. I am reminded that a mob toppled a lead statue of George III that was standing in Battery Park during the Revolution. They brought the pieces of lead to Wilton and made most of them into rifle balls; that is, all but one of the legs, and that leg is part of the plumbing in some house in the village, though I don't know which one.

Old Pot Luck loves to run to the barn. I give him his head, and for just a short run I feel that rhythm and speed and joy of being one with a horse, which is how it must feel for Nell because she rides so well. Back in the barn I curry, comb, and blanket old Pot Luck. I wonder how he likes being a gelding, or whether he knows or cares, and what he would be like if he were a stallion instead of an it.

Mrs. Norton is alone in the kitchen. The smell of cooking and baking is all about, and the dining-room table is set. Everybody else is dressing for dinner and a nauseous burn has come to my stomach, and I'm smelling all horsey. So I shower, shave, put on clean clothes—slacks, coat, and tie—and step out of my room at the top of the stairs and listen to the voices below. Chatter and laughter and the tinkle of glasses.

Here goes.

My usual beer is set out on a tray on the desk alongside the whiskey and gin, but today it's whiskey for me.

The flavor of Scotch always reminds me of neoprene or burning rubber. I settle into a chair with whiskey in hand and try to listen and join in and partake and contribute and be witty and bright while trying to drink the knot out of my stomach. My voice reaching higher and higher on the verge of hysteria and sounding to me like Donald Duck, and my head reeling mildly from whiskey. While one hand holds glass and feeds the mouth, the other is wiping a sweaty palm against the thigh and then switches glass to wipe the other palm.

But the conversation is animated and sparkling and we move into the dining room. The turkey is carved and served and I look at the plate piled high with white meat, creamed onions and turnips and beans and cranberry sauce and stuffing and gravy. How the hell will I ever eat this and be bright and turn the conversation in the direction that will lead to the declaration.

Nell is all smiles and grins at Mamma telling a story about a little black boy in her Head Start class, and I realize that the declaration, if it is to be made, must be made without introduction, because it needs none. I reach for my water glass as Pop begins to tell the story of Stanley Nelson nailing us at the station. I put down the glass and interrupt, "Folks . . . Mamma . . . Pop—"

Pop stops and looks. All eyes are on me, and my mouth is dry, and my heart is pounding. I take a deep breath and say, "Please pass the butter!"

They stare at me. Nell is shaking her head and looking down. Mamma passes the butter and looks at Pop and mercifully tells him to go on. He talks and describes and tells and all the while I'm holding the butter and wondering. I look at Nell, she's grinning. I could kill her. Mamma is intent on Pop who's having a good time with his story and a little high and not noticing I'm frozen solid holding the butter. He's reaching for a roll and stops midway and looks up, "Stanley? . . . Hell, no! He's at Vassar!" Pop lets out a roar and settles back in his chair laughing and looking around to see the effect.

"Folks . . . Nell and I want to get married." Done.

"What?" as the smile fades from his face.

"We want to get married."

"You and Nell?"

"Yes."

"To who . . . to whom?"

"To each other."

He looks at me, then to Nell, then to Mamma, then to Nell, and back to me.

"Is this some kind of a prank . . . because, if it is, I don't think it's very funny."

I put the butter down and tighten up and try to explain. "It's no joke, Pop, we want to get married."

He looks at Nell, and again to Mamma and pushes his chair back from the table and lets fly.

"Now just slow down, fella . . . You've just come back from two years in the bush and the tribal customs are a little different around here than what you've been used to." He looks at Mamma. "Sarah?"

She's put her fork down and is looking at Nellie and

then back at me. "I'm flabbergasted. I simply don't know what to say."

"I know what to say. No! I can think of seventy-eight reasons why it's a bad idea, not the least of which is the most obvious. You are brother and sister. Not blood relatives, of course, but siblings and I presume rivals . . ."

I break in, "You're afraid of what people will say."

"I don't give a damn what people will say! I'm thinking only of what your marrying Nell might do to yourselves, and most of all to this family if it doesn't work."

Nellie is mad at this last sally and slams down her spoon and quietly says: "It will work."

Then Mamma comes back: "The odds are not that good for marriages made in heaven, and this one would have been made at home . . ."

Pop breaks in saying that that's another thing and how I hardly ever knew any other girl, and I tell him I know lots of other girls and took out lots of them at college, which ticks him off, and makes him say that taking out a girl is a hell of a lot different than knowing them and understanding them enough to make a lifetime commitment and claim them as a wife.

"And furthermore, the point is that you go up to Vermont to rescue your sister from a shattered romance with that boob of a lawyer . . ."

"Father!" says Nell.

". . . from that boob of a lawyer . . . and you're lonely or got hot pants from two years in the jungle and decide you're both in love. You caught her on the rebound, Sam."

"No!"

He reaches for his wine. I try to bring forth all the tidy arguments I'd been rehearsing for this moment, but my mind boggles as my blood pressure mounts; I stammer and ramble on and on about how the thing that Nell and I have just discovered is pure and alive and has been there since we were tiny kids. I stumble and fumble and look to Mamma for some kind of support when Nell cuts through the brush. "Let me take this opportunity to say one thing . . ."

But Pop steps right on her words and bellows, "You kids today move too fast! Think the world is one big slot machine that pays off every time you pull the crank. Well, let me tell you, Samuel Barnes, the jackpot has been a long time coming for your mother and me. And you'll never know the close calls we've had along the way. But we did it!" Slamming his fist on the table. "We did it. We have made a family. A good, solid, old-fashioned, rock-ribbed, God-fearing family. And we haven't stuck together on this one piece of turf under this patched roof for all these years to see the whole thing torn apart when you step off an airplane one fine day and decide you're going to marry your sister."

All this time my head is face down over the plate, and I'm watching gravy ooze over cranberry sauce and wondering why he is scolding.

"You're mad, Pop."

"Damn right, I'm mad."

"At what? Because I love Nellie? And because she loves me?"

He looks away from my stare and muses in a different tone.

"Your brother isn't here. And he should have something to say about this."

"Holy cow, Pop. I ain't going to marry Magruder!"

And with this he pushes himself away from the table and gazes out the window, hands in his pockets, jingling some change and looking off across the valley toward Drum Hill. I look at Nell who is looking down at her plate, arms folded, biting her lip. Then Pop turns back. "You are both full grown. You know and I know I can't stop you from doing any damn fool thing you want to. But that doesn't mean I have to like it."

It's quiet as four faces around the room are staring in different directions. I spin my water glass and break the silence.

"Why are you so mad?"

With this Pop looks down and gently kicks a tassel on the rug. Turning slightly and croaking with a bitterness I've never heard from this man, he says, "Because I think something's going on!"

"George!" That's all Mamma says.

That's all anybody says. Pop walks out of the room, and Mamma follows after looking at each of us for a moment, offering a noncommittal gaze which may or may not contain the germ of an apology.

I look at Nell, and she at me, and what passes between us is not that mingling of matched feelings. I think she must believe I've blown it.

"He's mad, Nell. What next?"

"It will take time, but Mamma hasn't had her say. Nor have I had mine."

Without her having to say it, I know that Nell will want some quiet time with Mamma, and I know for sure I want to be away from everybody for a while. So Nell zips me into my corduroy jacket, and I head down Hill Road with the wind at my back. I sift through what I said and what he said and what I should have said instead and what I should have answered when he said such and such and wonder why Mamma didn't jump into the thing before she did. Of course I realize now, after the fact, that she jumped in as she always does when she is needed to cool and correct. How smart she is to be able to choke a careening argument with just a single word.

By putting one foot in front of another for a couple of miles and not thinking too much about which way I'm headed, I find myself standing on the bridge over the Norwalk River. Just up river from the bridge is the Benbow house, which is not really a house but an old mill that Clare Benbow got—a real steal—from a public-relations man who spent a lot of money fixing it up. His hysterical wife made him sell it right after the river came in the back door during the flood of sixty-five.

It can be no coincidence that I'm here. I might blame it on gravity, but I know that a more subtle machinery is at work. I feel pretty beat up, bent over, and confused, and Mrs. Clare Benbow always had a knack for making things seem better. Another thought occurs as I approach the door. Clare Benbow is my friend. And now I find that Magruder the Intruder has put himself in the scene by way of Meg. But, of course, I'm too old to harbor such petty jealousies.

It's rude to break in on Thanksgiving Day, but on the other hand I've been away and Meg did ask me to stop by soon and what the hell, maybe they're not at home, so I knock.

For just a second a blank stare, and then her face lights up. The next moment I'm sitting in a big overstuffed chair with my feet on the table and a beer in my hand and Clare is sitting on the sofa, legs tucked under her ass, puffing away on a long cigarette and laughing her lusty, hoarse laugh and nodding and listening and telling and asking and regaling like old times. Meg darts in with a crock of cheese, and of course eventually the Gruder's name enters the conversation, at which point Meg rushes off somewhere and comes back with a sheaf of papers which I'm instructed to read while she fills my glass. Limericks and naughty ditties that the Gruder has executed and sent back to Meg. Some are not bad and others are looney. I devour them fast as part of my search for a zinger and laugh out loud several times, Clare asking me to read the funny ones to her, and laughing again, and Meg taking the sheaf and picking out her favorites and reading. And as she reads she lays the pile face down on the coffee table in front of me, until I notice on the back of one of the sheets four lines written in Magruder's big, sweeping swirl. And while Meg is reading aloud and laughing, I try to make out the words of the four handwritten lines from the distance. Four lines not intended for my eyes. She has finished and Clare is laughing and I'm trying to laugh with them. In the moment of pause before Meg covers the lines and takes them away my eyes have a split-second feast of the writing. It evokes a feeling I've never seen put into words and I know in an instant that the zinger is there. It's there and it's gone. I will not ask this girl to let me read four lines not intended for me, but written by Magruder to the girl that he loves. *But* if I get out of here soon enough, the words might form in my mind.

Climbing the hill toward home, I try to move the words back and forth this way and that, but I can't make anything fit. It had something to do with a quote from John 14:2: "In my father's house are many mansions. . . ."

And then it went on for three lines, and the gist of it had to do with how each of them could be filled with joy. I wonder which of the lines contains the zinger and figure the easiest way to get it is to kid it out of Magruder when he gets back.

As I walk into the driveway, the setting sun is stabbing icy rays through the old oak. Nellie is closing the barn after putting Pot Luck down for the night, and she doesn't see me yet. She looks up and rolls a soft smile, and we meet right there under the oak by the kitchen window. I take her in my arms and kiss her and hug her and kiss her again, hoping they are watching.

For supper everybody raids the icebox and stacks the dishes in the sink. The rest of the evening everybody avoids everybody else, speaks in whispers and walks softly, and closes doors gently. While I'm sitting in bed and thumbing through Magruder's Bible looking for that passage in John, the owner of my father's house comes into one of its many mansions. To spread joy, I wonder? But he speaks softly and says only, "We will sleep on it, Sam." And just before leaving, he turns back for a moment, "I'm sorry for what I said. I'm sorry, Sam."

I need to level with him. I need to level and not to hurt. And an idea occurs. "What you said didn't bother me, Pop. It's what you feel that stings."

He pauses a moment by the open door, and I try to read his face but cannot tell whether the message was perfectly interpreted. He stands there in his baggy pj's with the old tattersall robe hanging loosely from his shoulders and slowly shuffles toward my bed. I brace for something that's going to happen—a hard swipe across the face. I will not duck. I will not flinch, goddamn it, if it will make him feel better. I close my eyes and wait and then feel his big hand tousle my head and go away for a moment. He flicks the light switch off and his hand returns to my head. But in the darkness it misses my hair and lands softly on my face. He must feel the wetness there. And he is gone.

Chapter

Twenty-two

Mamma's note left on the kitchen table explains that they have gone to Sharon Hospital to visit Uncle Spencer who just had another coronary. Uncle Spence is a retired Wall Street broker who raises setters and, every two years or so, gets hit with these things. Everybody rallies around the oxygen tent to hear the last words, and then pretty soon he's out running his dogs at field trials all over the state. The note tells me that there is coffee in the pot, which I'm already drinking, and that there is a sticky bun in the oven, which I'm already eating. It asks me to run some errands in the village and to please put some oats and water and hay in the stable and remember to lock the front door when I go out. And it says that there is still some cold turkey in the icebox if I get hungry and that they will be back by two and not later than three.

I saw them back out of the driveway from my bedroom. Three in the front seat of the Blue Debris. Nellie at the wheel. And now I'm alone and it's quiet. So quiet. Standing alone in an abandoned house. Yet somehow I don't mind the quality of this loneliness in this house. I walk slowly from the kitchen to the dining room and play some scenes that happened long ago and move on to the living room and look out across the valley and play some more scenes. I go into the library and run through the funny scene when Pop was telling me about girls and then go upstairs to the spare room that has the bed that Magruder claims has a mattress filled with cinder blocks. This is where Nell and I will sleep when we come back for visits. I go into Mamma's room to play a near-death scene with a happy ending and then past my room and Gruder's, saving Nellie's room for last. Déjà vu. For just eight, ten or maybe twelve seconds, some of the rapture returns. But this time I do not steal away. I pause to caress the carelessly tossed, pretty pink things and feel the pillow in the unmade bed and smell the perfume. I lie face down in the unmade bed and bury my face in her pillow and inhale the essence of Nellie Barnes.

Chapter

Twenty-three

"So here's the way it looks to Mamma and me in the cold light of day." He's saying this as we're seated around the kitchen table, Pop, Nellie, and me. Mamma's spooning warmed-over turkey and gravy onto our plates and Pop's pouring slightly corked wine.

"Number one—you quit college. You still don't know why but you got three-fourths of the way through and quit. Number two—you joined the Peace Corps and now that it's all over you think that was a mistake. Number three—you have your heart set on being a photographer and suddenly decide, no, you don't want that."

I'm forming counterarguments and about to explain

away each of these zigs and zags, and manage to get as far as "But . . ."

"Hear me out. It would be one thing if you wanted to marry some girl and you didn't have any kids and the thing didn't work out. Only two people could get hurt. But Nell hasn't had an easy time of it the past few years, and you, Sam, can't seem to fix on any set course. You two kids marrying . . . well . . . it doesn't have much of a chance. And when it breaks up, everything could break up. Everything. And if you have kids . . . and then it breaks up . . . I don't want to think about it. We're against it, Sam." The doorbell rings and Pop looks at Nell. He is cross and says, "See who that is." He shakes his head, "It's a dumb idea. Stupid."

As Nell gets up to go, Mamma tries to heal the breach and cool the argument. "I think we should suspend further discussion. Live with the idea for six months . . . or a year."

Nell is standing by the door to the hall. The bell rings again, and she says, "Let me take this opportunity to say one thing. *I love Sam Barnes.* I've known lots of boys and I love Sam. I've spent too long trying to convince myself I could love others. *But I love Sam!* And I won't be talked out of it."

The bell rings again and she leaves. Pop is muttering now and looking out the window. As Mamma is about to speak, Pop interrupts, ". . . whole younger generation going up in smoke. Pot!"

"Oh, come on Pop! What the hell does that have to do with us and loving each other?"

"Love? What do you know about love and marriage and commitment for a lifetime . . . you quit college . . ." Nell stands in the doorway, a ghastly, white pallor on her face that is drawn in a mask of agony. She is carrying a yellow paper. She puts it down beside me and gasps, "Gruder," and emits a sickening wail as she lurches out of the room. I hear her stumble on the stairs, and I look at Pop and Mamma rising, with stricken expressions, coming behind me, and taking the paper. He's dead. I hear Mamma scream behind me and Pop trying to comfort her with weak words. I feel their eyes piercing into my back as I sit frozen, my hands gripping the bottom of the chair, not moving but praying they don't notice that Samuel Thayer Barnes is alive and well and living at home, having successfully, for twenty-three years, looked out for Number One.

"He was just a little boy . . . a little boy," she cries and sobs. I can hear Pop leading her away and mumbling to me in a voice from the edge of a wide open grave, "Look after Nell, Sam."

And they're gone and I bolt from the table and the scene is blurred, but my eyes are dry as I burst through the back door and lean against the side of the house, and it all comes up—enzyme and turkey and onions and wine, and it goes on my shoe and into my nose and the red wine is all mixed and half-digested in the swimming slop, and I see this picture of a Man holding a cup and he's saying, "Take ye this in remembrance of Me," and I retch some more, but there's no more to puke. There are strings of slime hanging out of my mouth, and I wipe them off with my sleeve and look around for some-place to go. To hide.

Everything is quiet, and the world doesn't know or doesn't care that the Gruder is dead. A squirrel dashes across the lawn and he's alive and the oak is alive, and the grass is alive, and the bushes and birds and old Pot Luck and me, I'm alive. But the Gruder's dead, and there's no place to hide.

They will find me in the barn, and I can't take a car because they don't belong to me. But there is a rope still swinging from the treehouse, and if it's strong I'll hide there, and if it's not, I'll fall.

But it's strong, and I crouch on the weakened floor and peer out the window toward the house to see if any-one living there saw me climb up. It's still, and I wonder what they are saying and thinking, and I wonder about Nellie Barnes and what she thinks of me now. It's cold so I squat leaning against the trunk of the tree and let an emptiness creep into my gut and spread through my chest and down to my loins.

Suddenly I'm angry and there is nothing to punish and nothing to do. I kick a loose timber-slat on the side of the house, and it doesn't yield. It doesn't yield and I kick again and again; I'm mad, and I kick with my puke-covered shoe and it flies to the ground and I kick an-other and take it with bare hands and tear and rip and push and kick another and turn to a beam and twist it loose and push the whole side of the treehouse to the ground. The roof is hanging loose and I push it over and push and smash and tear and rip and kick and pick up a beam and shatter the floor and another beam resists my kick and the bash of my body and I pry it loose with a two-by-four and nearly fall as I watch them plummet to the ground. And the treehouse is gone.

Alone in the crotch of the old oak, I breathe fast, and I'm covered with sweat that chills my face. I'm cold as a corpse. There's no feeling in my body. It's empty and somewhere else. My mind is numb and far away. I hear children laughing and shouting and running and the cry of a child, "Wait, Sam, wait . . . Please wait!" And I hear the reply, "Get lost . . . get lost . . . get lost," and feel nothing. I look down and there on the lawn below and very far away is Nellie Barnes in her poplin raincoat with the collar turned up against the cold looking up at me, and I hear her voice; "When are you coming down?" She walks to one side for a better view. "I'm upset too, you know. You aren't the only one."

She stands there shivering and pleading with her eyes. I remember her now from the time way back when I could love her, and she could love me. I must explain to her as best I can what will be. "I can tell you this, Nellie. I have three things to do. I shall bury my brother. I shall locate your parents. And then get lost. L-o-s-t. Lost!"

"And you and me?"

"Nellie. That was my bullet. Mine. My bullet. Don't you see?"

"No."

"I was never meant to be. And I am. Magruder was meant to be. And he is not."

"But the Polliwog Speech. You taught me that's not right . . . and that's not right . . ." She tarries and looks up and shivers and turns her back and then walks head down toward the house.

After a while a car drives up, and the doctor goes into the house. I watch a light go on in Mamma's room, and then the light goes out, and the doctor is standing below and looking up talking to me. Finally he walks to his car and drives away, and the stillness leaves as the light diminishes, and the wind brings life to the dark.

Chapter

Twenty-four

I walked out of the bathhouse and onto the beach and a woman looked up and stared and got out of the way and a child ran off to its mother and clutched and then other people were staring, and they began to laugh and point, and I came up to Nellie and Magruder and Mamma and Pop, and they looked and laughed, and then other people gathered around and stared and pointed and laughed, and I looked down and saw that I was wearing no trunks and down in my loins where once there had been fire now there was nothing but ashes. And they stopped laughing and started to curse and shove and taunt and push and drive me off, and I was glad to be gone, and covered up and concealed.

Chapter

Twenty-five

Nellie helped Pop work out the details. They selected the hymns and pallbearers and arranged for the flowers. They asked young Stanley Nelson to write and read a eulogy (and the subject he chose was courage, Sam), notified friends, and arranged a reception at the house. Nell comforted the old folks and even notified Jawbreakian's secretary that I would be unable to start right away—this was a half-lie because I didn't intend to start. Period.

And she selected the gravesite beside which we are standing now, Pop beside Mamma, and me beside Nell. Maybe a hundred young kids, boys and girls, are coming up the hill and standing sort of back from the hole, waiting as they unload the box that's covered by the em-

blem of the United States of America. The whole thing
reminds me of some kind of macabre pep rally. Victory
hymns and Stanley's speech about all of us being
different for having known him, and his spirit enduring
in our hearts. Then I notice a covey of soldiers carrying
rifles and getting themselves organized around the box,
which the bearers are about to bring to the grave. I
think about that neatly typed and hurriedly signed form
letter that came on White House stationery and about
the idiocy of shooting off guns over the corpse of someone killed by a gun and thank you, Mr. Commander-in-
Chief, you've done quite enough and you can go back
to your *Reader's Digest* now, and I break away from the
family and walk quickly down the hill and stop the startled procession and turn to the sergeant in charge and
tell him right off, "You can go."

The sergeant is bewildered and stands there staring
and looking about and staring back. "But . . . regulations . . ."

"Fuck your regulations . . . he's ours now. Do you
hear? Take your guns and get out."

He nods to his buddies, and they are gone, and I take
the handle at the end of the box, and we walk up the
hill and put it in the ground.

I am driving the Green Debris with Nell beside me
and the folks in back. They are talking about who was at
the church—who this one was and that one—and about
the prep school roommate named Coco who flew in
from Seattle and about the three black kids from Mam-

ma's Head Start school who came. Everybody's missing the point.

We get to the driveway and are walking up the front walk. Mamma is clutching the emblem like it was a baby. She stops and looks at me. "Sam, I want you to put up this flag." She holds it out to me, and through her black veil I see her dry eyes and wonder how or why she wants to honor this present from the faceless eunuchs who sit around the White House basement describing parameters and deciding who shall live and who shall die while they are slipping and sliding and zigging and zagging and reaching for power and glory.

"Not now. Not now I won't."

"Put it up, Sam."

"I'll burn it."

"Samuel Thayer Barnes. I'm glad you chased off those soldiers, but right now I want you to run up my flag." She says "my flag" like it was her flag, her very own flag, forgetting it is *Their* flag too, and forgetting that if you honor your very own flag, you are also honoring theirs and them and this is wrong to do.

I'm thinking of all these things and all the things she's suffered. There is no time to explain or debate, and she goes on, "If it's to be burned, I'll burn it!" and she thrusts it into my hands. "But you've got to make it fly."

I look about, and all the friends and relatives and Stanley and Coco and the other people are standing around and waiting and watching Mamma and me. I walk across the lawn and lock the clips into the eyelets and carefully uncleat the halyard and, taking care that the flag doesn't touch the ground, pull and unfurl and hoist it to the top of the pole and then cleat the halyard and turn to see everybody watching it wave. Mamma and Pop and Nellie looking at it for a moment and then walking toward the house.

Chapter

Twenty-six

The man was only going as far as Rahway, so I stand by the river waiting for another ride and think that when I die this is the place where my ghost will come to live. The chemical plant is spilling slime, heat, and crud into the river, and the land is covered with cinders. The factory stacks billow black and red smoke into the gray December sky, and the flares from the cracking plants burn an eternal flame in tribute to what this all once was and never can be again.

It must have been a scene such as this that inspired my conception in the back seat of some four-door sedan in a hidden lovers' lane all littered with beer cans and wet rubbers, one warm spring night, twenty-three years and eleven months ago. The dark side of the Polliwog

Speech. If it's my heritage, I accept it and must be glad for it and make of it what can be made. But the evil thus derived, though it cannot be contained or eliminated except by means that I lack the courage to implement, can indeed be isolated. And this shall be done.

A man named Theisiger was born in the Sudan of British parents and lived there during his young life and then went to Cambridge. On leaving, he set out to test himself by living among the Bedouin Arabs, eating what they ate and wearing what they wore and several times crossing the Rub al Khali on foot with small camel caravans. A thousand miles of empty sands and sometimes weeks between waterholes. In that desolation there is no data bank or file cabinet or records or black-ribboned envelopes or dossiers or newspaper morgue. Yet a Bedouin can tell, by examining the tracks in the shifting sands, the clumps of half-eaten weeds and the droppings of long-departed camels, who has passed this way, when and how many there were and what was their sex and where they were going, how much they were carrying, whether an animal had a sore leg or was carrying calf, and what their food was and how much water they had. Instant data retrieval system.

There is no such comparable skill in existence in the United States of America. In its place is the FBI and the IRS and the Census Bureau and on and on down to the county, municipal, town and district record offices. The people who gather the data are called bureaucrats, and they don't understand the data they keep nor do they understand that it is not just data carefully kept and carelessly contemplated, but that it is all that is left of events and happenings and celebrations of the pageant of life.

I was on to something in the library at Princeton and called Nellie collect to tell her to meet me in Trenton City Hall. And all she replied was "to hell with it. Come home." I told her, "Someday maybe" and rang off.

The break comes at 3:05 p.m., in drawer 732, file 86, in the Bureau of Records, City of Trenton, County of Mercer. The name was the same as the one scrawled on the back of the Haverman envelope, and it was easy to trace the begats down through two hundred years and cross-check with the Bureau of Motor Vehicles and find three persons with the same surname and select from the dates of birth the most likely to sire a foundling in the Year of Our Lord 1949.

I slam the drawer shut and there in the basement of room 8-B in the Bureau of Records in the County of Mercer in the State of New Jersey is Nellie Barnes. Smiling. Telling how she was stopped by a left-handed cop for making a left-hand turn from a right lane. The cop had forgotten his pen and his ticket book turned out to be a Zen paperback, and he had known Martha Wheeler when she was at Smith and he was at Harvard and he had been with her when she was in Chicago in '68 and been busted for smashing her two hundred-dollar guitar over the blue-helmeted head of one of Chicago's Finest. And his name was Officer Wright, but everybody called him Lefty. Symmetrical.

She shrugs when I ask how she knew where to find me

and I hand her the paper with the things I've been copy-ing.

"I found something. It's all right here. A church in Bayonne. They should know where your mother is . . . well . . . take it. Don't you want it?"

"No! I want to take you home."

"I'm leaving. I can get a bus from here . . . maybe to Denver or L.A. . . . who cares? When I get there and things get sorted out, I'll drop you a postcard. Here. Take the paper and don't lose it. What the hell is the matter with you, Sis? Take it."

"I don't need that. Nor do I care about it anymore. I just want you to come home."

"I'm going to miss the bus, Nell . . ." and I take the paper and thrust it into her hand. We stand silently there in Room 8-B.

She turns ever so slightly, and I can see just the back of her head and part of her soft cheek and lashes and nose as she unfolds the paper and looks down. It's the girl on the deck with her chin held high, hair blowing, with a trace of a smile. I loved her.

"But, Sam, I don't know where this is . . . I don't know how to find it." And turning back to face me, "Please Sam . . . before you go . . . there'll be an-other bus."

We're back in the Green Debris, speeding through the Jersey flats, hanging a right at Elizabeth, and taking

the toll bridge to Bayonne. We drive among the funnels
and plumbing of the petrochemical works, back lots,
coal piles, junkyards, tarpaper two-family houses with
postage-stamp yards with galvanized steel fences, pink
plaster flamingoes, and bird baths, and past boarded-up
storefronts with the tattered remains of posters of defeated Polish politicians, and past Elks clubhouses with
glass brick windows and past secondhand furniture
stores. We come to a stop. Standing alone in the middle
of two empty lots is a brick church painted red with an
attached parish house. The lots are littered with the car-
casses of washing machines and are bordered on one
side by the backwater tributary of the Bayonne Canal,
and on the other by a paint-factory warehouse and great
silver drums with a sign reading *Humble.*

I wait for her at the edge of the canal and survey the
wreckage of progress and wonder what kind of life can
grow from the decay of all this. I watch the tiny bubbles
of some odious gas pop to the surface of the still and
slimy waters that once spawned fish and was a haven for
game and cleansed the bodies of bare-assed kids and led
downstream to a river and out to a great clean ocean,
and I am ashamed that I'm a child of this time.

Nellie is standing on the steps of the parsonage and
looking about. She sees me and is coming over, and I
move to her to tell her to take me to the bus in Newark.

"Are you glad you went in?"

"She died . . . some time ago."

"I'm sorry. You found out nothing else?"

"I didn't ask. It was like you said it would be. The spooks never were. Now there's only you and me. Take me home."

"Drop me off in Newark."

I break away and start the long, slow walk toward the Green Debris, Nell following close behind, and then she's running ahead of me, backwards facing me, her eyes flashing, "I love you, Sam. I love *you*. You taught me . . ."

"Nonsense, we just had a little fun."

And now she's alongside me, "Besides, Nellie, there's the matter of parental consent."

"They're testing us, Sam, the way any parent would do. We have to convince them. Sam, we have to fight."

I'm walking and thinking how impenetrable are the will and reason of the fixed and emotionally committed mind and how difficult it is to find the precise word that has the power to open the curtain and reveal the world as it is and must be.

She has run in front of me and stopped me cold. "Sam, you love me. Look me in the eye and tell me you don't."

This is too much. I reach out and take the lapels of her poplin raincoat, the same one that was open and blowing in the wind when there was just a trace of a smile on her face and I loved her.

"I'm looking you in the eye and telling you I can't. Are you blind? You put a telegram on the table and ran out. You weren't there after that. You didn't see them

. . . the two of them . . . reading and crying and looking at me. You think I don't know what they were
thinking. I got found out! Me, sitting at their table all
smug and sassy and alive and him . . . splattered over
half of Asia!"

And I let go and turn away.

"You think . . . you can't believe they despise you
because you're alive? What kind of people do you think
we are? Magruder's dead."

"Oh, Nellie . . ."

"We loved him . . . but he's not coming back."

"Me either."

"He brought joy to our lives. He taught us to laugh
and sing. And, Sam, do you know he loved you most of
all?"

Now searching my face and saying it again. "He loved
you most of all, Sam, don't let him down!"

I cannot let her see what these words do to me. I
must turn away and start toward Los Angeles and the
oceans beyond.

He did. He really did. He loved me most of all. And I
walk faster and faster through the rain toward the
Green Debris.

"That's self-pity, Sam. Self-pity." And now screaming:
"You quit! You quit! Quitter! Quitter! You quit!"

Anger floods into my veins and I must stop and con-
front this assault on my reason and sensibility, here in
this wasteland where her words reverberate against the
warehouse walls. "I'll play back your own theme, Nellie.

Other people's feelings are involved. You forget that!"
These words lash from my tongue, and I turn to avoid
her stare and walk on.

But she's right. He did bring joy to our lives, and
taught us to laugh and sing, and the echo of his laughter
filled all the mansions of my father's house. And he
loved me most of all. But how my creed and my very
being repaid his love! I will say no more. But I wonder
about that line from Camus and about Magruder. Why
he did accept that invitation to death?

The rain is cold and is beginning to numb. She will
soon give up. Then we can go.

And I think of the Gruder and about his ghost and
where it will choose to visit and whom it will allow to
know it and be with and when. And of Mamma and
Pop and of the treasures they've nurtured and banked
only to have torn and splintered and destroyed. From
this destruction I must draw the consequences and
somehow transform them into a rule of life.

I know Nellie is behind me because I can feel her
presence. "Sam . . . you've mourned his death." And
then in a tone that is neither a cry nor a scream, but
rather a ringing chord that no other human voice could
form, she says, "Now, Sam . . . Now! . . . celebrate his
life!"

One word ricochets through the dark tunnels of my
mind, as if all the world were in darkness and suddenly a
blazing aurora illuminates from within all the cities of
my heart.

And slowly, here in a vacant lot in Bayonne, New Jersey, with the December rain pelting my face, and soaking my skin and half-blinding my eyes, and with the words of two night-given speeches sweeping through my brain and before me the blurred image of four lines of script containing the zinger and the picture of Pop standing red-faced and laughing on the lawn holding his side, and the vision of a young hand lofting gently to touch a bronze nose, I hear the faintest tone of an oboe sounding an A. And then a whole symphony reaching and finding and swelling the note and lifting a curtain for a concert about to begin. And I look up into the wet sky and let its rain mingle with mine and pause just a moment to find a reply, and it isn't there.

As I turn to my love who's standing head high, all wet and washed and grinning, and reaching for her all I can think of to say is, "This weather ain't even fit for ducks."